Aug. 2011

D1495458

True
Believers

Linda Dorrell

True Believers

A NOVEL

Baker Books

A Division of Baker Book House Co
Grand Rapids, Michigan 49516

Published by Baker Books
a division of Baker Book House Company
P.O. Box 6287, Grand Rapids, MI 49516-6287

Printed in the United States of America

ISBN 0-7394-1899-8

This is a work of fiction. All characters, incidents, and places either are products of the author's imagination or are used fictitiously. Any resemblance to actual persons, living or dead, or actual events is entirely coincidental.

For my mother,
Kathleen Meekins Dorrell

Thank you
for teaching me to believe

I have desired to go
　　Where springs not fail,
To fields where flies no sharp and sided hail
　　And a few lilies blow.

And I have asked to be
　　Where no storms come,
Where the green swell is in the havens dumb,
　　And out of the swing of the sea.

from "Heaven-Haven"
by Gerard Manley Hopkins

Daylilies grew wild in the ditches around Bonham, and Peggy Nickles thought the bright orange ones would add a festive air to the house. She stood at the bay window, absentmindedly arranging a few of them in her mother's antique crystal vase. It was a sunny Wednesday morning in June, and she was waiting for her three sisters to arrive for their twice-a-month brunch, this being her week to host the small affair.

Their mother had died three years before, just one year after their father had fallen dead at his desk in the textile mill. He had inherited the mill, like his father and grandfather, and served as its president after his father's death. One day, his secretary had walked in and found him with his head down on the desk, like a school child who had fallen asleep in class. A half hour later she realized he hadn't moved at all.

Brokenhearted and unused to coping alone, their mother had found a bottle of old sleeping pills and swallowed them deep in the night on the one-year anniversary of his death. Since then, Peggy and her sisters had made the brunches a ritual, a way to hang on to one another and keep themselves, if not close, at least acquainted.

Peggy had laid out the dining room table with a fresh damask tablecloth and white linen napkins. Crystal goblets sparkled at each place set with pale blue salad plates featuring a pattern of white roses. The centerpiece, like the window arrangement, featured orange daylilies. Peggy fretted that she couldn't get white roses to grow profusely, the way her mother had in that luxurious rose garden of hers. How fragrant it had been: tea roses, English roses clambering up trellises, perfuming the June air with their intoxicating fragrance. They were her mother's pride, her gift. Peggy longed for those roses—they would have accented the china well.

The oven timer buzzed, and Peggy darted in to check the biscuits. Eva, the eldest sister, always insisted on freshly baked tea biscuits at brunch, no matter who entertained. It did not matter if the cook had a knack for baking or not. Eva ate them whether they had the texture of school paste, the consistency of caramel candy, or the crumbly quality of wedding cake.

Today they were perfect. Peggy had worked long and hard to make the biscuits correctly. Doing anything correctly, whether it was baking, gardening, decorating, or hanging out the laundry, was essential and required in Peggy's family. She placed the hot pan on the kitchen table and styled the biscuits into a neat pyramid on an antique china platter that matched the table service. Hearing the front door creak, she whipped off her apron and stuffed it in the pie safe.

"It's me, Peggy," Eva called out, striding into the hallway.

"You're always early," Peggy complained, aiming a kiss at Eva's cheek but missing when her sister pulled up short.

"Punctuality is a virtue," Eva replied. Eva was a strict immersion Baptist, as were all the Nickles sisters. Another family tradition, like belonging to the Junior Welfare League and the Bonham Country Club, serving on the Library Committee, or volunteering with the Butler County Hospital's Ladies Auxiliary. "Can I help with anything?"

"No, I'm almost ready." Peggy retrieved a plate of chicken sandwiches and pimiento cheese sandwiches from the icebox. She placed them on the dining room table where she had already laid out a platter of chilled, sliced tomatoes, tomato aspic, and a jar of peach marmalade. She surveyed the table and remembered her manners. "How is Gail?"

"Dying to come stay with you." Eva plopped her purse on the corner of the table, rattling the dishes, and sat down heavily.

"So let her. I'd be glad to have her. It does get kind of lone-some out here sometimes." Peggy loved her niece, enjoyed spending time with her. Now that she was twelve, Gail was at that awkward age, between toys and boys, and often needed to confide in someone other than her mother, who could be judg-mental and unyielding, or her friends, who were too immature to offer advice.

"Her summer needs to be spent more constructively than wasting time out here in the middle of nowhere." Eva sniffed.

Peggy stopped pouring tea. "I know I made it sound deso-late, but it's not like I'm cut off from civilization."

The screen door slammed on the middle hallway. "Did you think we weren't coming?" Belva said, followed by Beatrice. Both were peeling off white gloves. Belva and Beatrice were twins, and even at the age of forty-two, they insisted on dress-ing identically. Today they wore red polka-dot dresses with broad, starched white collars, accessorized by red leather hand-bags and red and white spectator pumps.

"Nice outfits," Eva said, rolling her eyes.

"Thank you," they answered in unison.

"I just *love* your new car, Peggy," Beatrice drawled, pulling back the curtains and admiring the gleaming powder-blue Cadillac convertible. "Those fins are absolutely rakish!"

"Call me crazy," Peggy said, glancing around and feeling as if she had forgotten something. "I don't know what came over me. I'm usually not one to go in for fads. I suppose it just cap-tivated me."

"Enough about the car," said Eva. "Let's eat."

They gathered around the table, sitting two on each side, always leaving the chairs at the ends empty, as if they were expecting their parents to arrive suddenly and find themselves displaced—unsituated, as it were.

"Say grace, Belva," Beatrice said. The sisters folded their hands on the edges of the table and bowed their heads.

"Dear heavenly Father, we thank you for your many bless-ings—the joys of family, the beatitude of heart, health, and home, the gift of your Son Jesus and his unselfish sacrifice on the cross for our mortal sins and souls. . . ."

Eva sighed and opened her eyes, catching Peggy staring out the window, her hands still folded.

"We beseech you to protect our loved ones from harm and hazard, our souls from eternal damnation, our hearts from temptation, and our bodies from carnal lust. . . ."

At this last, Beatrice opened her eyes and socked Belva solidly on the shoulder.

"Sister, God does not want to hear such talk at brunch."

Peggy, breaking her trance, began to giggle.

Belva looked around, casting a condemnatory eye on her sisters.

"Silence!"

The room went dead quiet. It was as if their mother had spoken from the grave.

"In all these things we beseech you, making our prayers and petitions known. We also ask that you bless this food of which we are about to partake for the sustenance and nourishment of our earthly bodies. In Jesus' name we pray, Amen."

"Amen!" the sisters echoed. Peggy tried to hide her smile. Belva had a way of getting wound up in a prayer and not being able to find her way out.

"What is with you, Peggy?" Eva said, daintily picking up one biscuit, then another. "You were staring out that window like you were seeing a ghost."

"Maybe I was," Peggy said, passing the dish of marmalade. She placed her napkin in her lap. "Isn't a woman allowed to daydream?"

"You are thirty-six years old. Your daydreaming days are over," Eva said, placing a chicken sandwich on her plate and cutting it diagonally with her knife.

"I knew nothing would come of this," Belva said, staring at the tomato aspic.

"I made that from your recipe," Peggy said, grabbing the plate and examining the congealed mass closely.

"Not that," Belva said, snatching it back and serving herself a slender slice. "This, this . . . this place."

"What's wrong with it?"

Peggy looked around. She felt content in the cottage, cozy and safe. Built during the 1920s, it was well constructed, although she had replaced some plumbing already. For a small house, it had spacious rooms. She had decorated the long central hallway with family portraits inherited from her parents. Her sisters found the images facing out from the old tintypes stern and dour, but Peggy saw within them a sense of continuity, as if she could look at the faces and somehow divine their lives and thoughts. She hung the old frames carefully in family groups, according to ancestral line, creating a generational tableau that comforted her and fascinated Gail.

"I love this house," Peggy said, rising to look out the window.

"We are not talking about the house, Peggy," Belva said.

"We are talking about that spooky old boneyard," Beatrice added.

"Whatever possessed you to buy a graveyard?" Eva said, shaking her head and slathering marmalade on yet another biscuit.

"I didn't buy the cemetery," Peggy said, peering through the lace-covered window. "At least not all of it. The deeds belong to the plot owners."

"Who are all dead," Beatrice said.

"In perpetuity," Belva added.

"It came along with the church and the manse. I guess you could call it a package deal." Peggy had gone through this discussion with her sisters before. It always came around to the graveyard.

After their parents died, each sister received a sizeable inheritance. Since Belva, Beatrice, and Eva were all married, their money usually went into whatever their husbands thought they should put it, although Eva managed to make clear her preferences on investments and savings. Still, this was 1954, and the men were, in the end, in charge. Peggy, however, being single, was under no such constraint. She saw the money as a means to do something she had wanted to do all her life.

Peggy Nickles wanted to own a church.

She didn't have the urge to preach or start a wayward religious sect or defy God by turning one of his houses of worship into a honky tonk. She simply liked the idea of having her own spiritual haven, a place where she could be alone with God, tell him her thoughts and dreams and fears. Her own slice of heaven was how she liked to think of it.

The congregants' descendants had abandoned the building, the cemetery, and the accompanying parsonage years ago, after the last congregant died in 1939. The pastor who served the church left to join the Army just in time to minister to the burgeoning force about to wash over Europe. It had fallen into disrepair, like unoccupied dwellings do, deteriorating from lack of love and care, and maintenance. Buildings, like people, need sustenance to survive, and it had disheartened Peggy to watch the simple dwelling and old-fashioned chapel become a shambles.

She had been to the church a few times as a young child, with her parents, to homecomings and weddings and funerals. Some of her ancestors had founded the church, and her parents still felt their own spiritual connection. But the pull of society had lulled them away from the simple country chapel, and the girls had grown up going to the big Baptist church in town.

Given to long hikes in the country, Peggy had run across the church one autumn day when leaves were cascading across the lonely dirt road that ran past it. Vines slithered up the sides of the edifice, and the trees and shrubs surrounding it had grown wild, nearly obliterating it from view. Often, Peggy would climb through an open window she had stumbled upon at the rear of the sanctuary. Inside, she would sit on a dusty pew, singing "In the Garden" or "Amazing Grace" aloud from a tattered hymnal and bathing in the pastel blue glow that emanated from the frosted windows. The chapel did not have stained glass— post–Civil War congregants could not afford such luxuries. Nevertheless, as Peggy sat there and sang, she imagined the windows replaced with soaring panes depicting glorious biblical tales in Technicolor, panes that would bathe her in rainbow light, the promise to Noah after the flood.

After indulging in her daydreams, Peggy usually wandered through the large, neglected cemetery, pushing back the weeds from time to time to read the old-fashioned inscriptions and epitaphs. She was particularly fond of, but saddened by, the children's graves. Bereaved parents had inscribed several of the tombstones "Budded on Earth to Bloom in Heaven." The tall, carved pillars placed there in honor of the more well-to-do members and their families also awed her. A few family crypts and plots dominated the section nearest the old sanctuary, while the more common folk were scattered between. Several monuments bore the designation CSA—Confederate States of America—in honor of the Civil War veterans interred beneath.

She couldn't stand to see the church fall into ruins. Milo Percy, the family attorney, checked the status of the property for her and found no reason she couldn't buy it. So she did.

"Peggy? Peggy!" Eva shook her arm. "Are you listening?"

"No, Eva, I'm not," Peggy said as she pushed back her chair. "To tell the truth, I've heard it all before. I am *not* getting rid of it." She began clearing the table.

"Well, no one is saying you have to get rid of the whole thing, dear," Belva said.

"Just the church and graveyard," said Beatrice.

"That's what I bought it for," Peggy said, sighing.

"Oh, nonsense," Eva exclaimed. "You are just doing this to disgrace Mother and Daddy's memory."

Peggy stopped on her way to the kitchen, her knuckles white as she gripped the treasured family china. "What gives you the right to accuse me of such a horrible thing? What in the world have I ever done to make you think I would do anything to dishonor their memory?" She began to shake and placed the dishes carefully on the buffet, resisting the temptation to hurl the stack at Eva.

"You never rebelled against them in life," Eva said matter-of-factly. "There was a lot of stuff pent up in you. It's coming out now."

"What's coming out?" asked Belva, puzzled.

"Her rebellious streak."

"I declare, she's been reading those awful psychology books again," Belva said. Beatrice nodded. "Pretty soon she'll be psychologizing us." Getting up from the table, she pulled at Eva's sleeve. "Come on, sister, let's go."

"I am not done yet." Eva grabbed the plate of biscuits.

"Yes, you are." Peggy leveled a raging stare at her eldest sister. "Go. Now. Stay out of my business. It is my church. It is my cemetery. And I intend to restore it all."

At this all three sisters stopped and regarded Peggy with apprehension.

"Peggy, you'll spend your entire inheritance resurrecting those old ruins," Beatrice said. "That is not what Daddy would have wanted."

"I don't know what Daddy would have wanted for me, and neither do you." Peggy smoothed her skirt and stood at the head of the table. "He never saw fit to tell me. He only told me what he didn't want for me. That was just about everything, and it almost worked out that way. But he's gone, I'm here, and I've got a church to restore." She resumed clearing the table.

"However will you do it?" Belva asked. "You're not used to that kind of labor. We're indoors people."

"I already have someone in mind," Peggy said.

"Who?" Eva stood and placed her hands on her hips. "I hope it's not that repulsive Yancy. He does fine work, but he stinks worse than a goat pen."

"No," said Peggy. "I've decided Otha Lee will help me."

Belva and Beatrice tittered. "That old colored preacher that used to work for Daddy?" Belva said. "He must be in his sixties by now."

"How in the world are you and one old man going to fix up a whole church?" Belva sat down again.

"Probably very slowly," Peggy said, "but it will all be for his benefit in the end."

"Whose benefit?" Beatrice asked, joining her twin at the table.

"Otha Lee's, of course."

"And why would that be?" Eva inquired, finally leaving the table and leaning against the doorpost.

"Because when I finish," Peggy said, turning to go into the kitchen, "I'm giving it to him." Belva and Beatrice gasped in unison.

Always the family skeptic, Eva rolled her eyes. "Giving it to him?"

"Yep. Graveyard and all."

Eva stalked into the hall, followed by the twins, who were arm-in-arm and whispering fiercely. "Call us when you've come to your senses!" Eva shouted, the screen door slamming behind her.

Peggy walked to the front door and watched her sisters get into their respective cars and zoom away on the dusty road. She stepped out onto the front porch and examined the church, which stood across the road.

"Dear Lord," she prayed. "I hope I'm doing the right thing. Although I have a feeling you'll let me know if I'm not."

Elder Otha Lee Sturgis, pastor of the Mount Gilead Missionary Baptist Church, sat back on the front porch of his run-down tar-papered shack and reflected on the words of the previous Sunday's sermon and pondered topics for next Saturday's evening service.

His small congregation was made up mostly of elderly ladies whose husbands had passed on long ago from the strain of sweltering summers in the tobacco, peanut, and cotton fields. Otha Lee himself bore the physical scars—the arthritic hands, the bent and bowed back. He could sense changes in the weather by his aching bones.

Otha Lee looked up from his Bible and thought about Paul's affliction, his "thorn," the messenger of Satan, and wondered if rheumatism qualified. His people had certainly suffered enough, but to have to deal with suffering as the result of other suffering nearly made him grieve and moan.

"'My grace is sufficient for thee,' saith the Lord," Otha Lee quoted aloud, his current congregation being the hens pecking peacefully in the front yard beneath the chinaberry tree. He pulled up his head to spot a blue Cadillac convertible peeling down the dirt road leading to his home. He stood, straightened his suspenders, and donned a tattered straw hat before ambling out to greet the driver.

"Why, Miss Peggy, what brings y'all way out here into no-man's-land?" he asked, tipping his hat and opening the car door for her.

"Visiting, Otha Lee," she replied brightly, brushing grit from her purse. "I was thinking about you and decided I'd just drive out and see how you're doing."

"I'm doing well, Miss Peggy, just fine. Even better now that Mr. Leonard Nickles' favorite child is here."

Peggy laughed. "Don't let my sisters hear you say that."

Otha Lee put his hand to his mouth as if turning a key.

Peggy cleared her throat. "To be truthful, Otha Lee, I came to make you a business proposition."

"Business with a preaching man?" Otha Lee scratched his head. "You ain't looking to make any deals with the Lord, are you now, 'cause he doesn't take bribes!"

At that, they both laughed. Otha Lee often made jokes with Peggy as she was growing up, a subtle way of poking fun at her father's propensity for making every encounter a potential opportunity to turn a profit.

"No deals with God. Or the devil, either, for that matter. Although that is what some people might say I'm fixing to do."

"Come on up here on the porch and sit," he said, gesturing to a faded rocking chair. "Now, what's on your mind, Miss Peggy?"

"You know I purchased the old church off Highway 6." Peggy settled into the creaky rocker. "It has turned out to be a little more than I expected work-wise."

"Yeah, I noticed that. Old cemetery's getting mighty sprangly."

"Yes, and it's not just that. It's the building itself. The floor's rotten, the windows are broken. It's full of dust, and birds are making nests in the hanging chandeliers."

"Mmmm, mmmm. Sounds like you got a real job ahead of you." Otha Lee took off his hat and fanned away a gnat. "Now, you mentioned something about a business proposition?"

"Hear me out before you give me an answer."

"I'm listening, Miss Peggy. Go on."

Peggy sat on the edge of the rocker, looking down at her skirt, then into Otha Lee's eyes.

"If you'll help me restore it, I'll give you the deed to the church."

Otha Lee thanked the Lord he was sitting. He fanned himself briskly.

"Bless your heart, Miss Peggy, but your daddy's turning over in his grave about now."

"Otha Lee, I know you don't have a proper church. You have a—what's it called—a brush arbor?"

"Yes, ma'am, and it works just fine."

"Unless it's raining or cold or snowing or 102 degrees. Am I right?"

"The Lord provides shelter from the heat and the cold and the driving rains in my flock's house."

"But wouldn't your flock be much more comfortable out of the weather?" Peggy studied the old man's face.

Otha Lee let out a deep sigh, then a booming laugh. "What you're saying is that you want a bunch of gospel-singing, drum-beating, foot-stomping, amening, hallelujahing, glory-be-to-God, holiness Negroes to move into a church that ain't held nothing but upstanding quiet white folks since Civil War times. A church that a Nickles—a white Nickles—owns." He stood and propped his leg on the sagging porch railing, resting his tattered black Bible on his knee.

"I can't look after it. I really don't know what I was thinking when I bought it." She grabbed Otha Lee's arm. "Please do not tell my sisters that."

Otha Lee knew Peggy's sisters well. He grinned broadly. "Don't you worry about that. Remember, I locked my lips up a few minutes ago. Your sisters won't hear it from me."

"I guess I was trying to preserve history, save the past. Maybe I thought that if I owned my own church I could go to whenever I wanted, I would find some real peace at last."

"Whatever your reasons were, it sounds like now you're looking to change history." Otha Lee glanced at her from the corner of his eye. "That is one way, I guess."

"Please tell me you'll think about it." Peggy picked up her purse and moved toward her car.

"I promise I won't be thinking about much else," he said, opening the door for her with a flourish.

"We'll talk again," Peggy said, backing up and raising another cloud of dust. "Pray about it!" she shouted.

Otha Lee wandered the yard, scattering the chickens. He had dreamed of his own church for years, ever since he had heard the call on the night lightning struck his parents' home, burning it to the ground. Of course Otha Lee knew in his heart it wasn't a lightning of the literal sort, but he always thought of it as lightning, nonetheless. His ma and pa, his three sisters, and his four brothers: all died. Otha Lee had been late returning home from his job tending the Nickles' tobacco curing barns and so was spared.

"'My grace is sufficient for thee,'" Otha Lee boomed over the hog pen. "'Amazing grace. How sweet the sound.'"

As Peggy drove away, her sisters' voices bounced around in her head. She wasn't sure if she had violated an unspoken protocol by going to Otha Lee's house, but she had felt confident the preacher would be attentive to her offer and would give it serious consideration.

Otha Lee had worked for Peggy's father for more than forty years, since he was a small boy. He had to find some way to make a life and a living for himself after his family was lost in the fire. Mr. Nickles had employed Otha Lee in various capacities over the years—driver, handyman, mechanic, field hand on the family farms. Yet he still allowed Otha Lee to attend school, receive an education. On occasion Leonard Nickles seemed to need Otha Lee as a spiritual advisor; that by his being spared from the fire, Otha Lee had been blessed in some special way that gave him a direct line to God.

Peggy had observed the men secretly when they were together, wondering at their strange friendship—almost a kinship, she often thought. Otha Lee sometimes came to the house, but Peggy could never remember either of her parents inviting

Otha Lee into the parlor or to a meal, even if he came at supper time. The cook and housekeeper seemed to look down on Otha Lee with a disdain Peggy could not understand.

Peggy reflected on this and decided she had done the right thing by asking Otha Lee to help her restore the church. He was a man of God, and he had been a right hand to her father. Why shouldn't the Nickles family reward him? Otha Lee had suffered mightily, not only losing his family at a young age but losing his wife later. She had died young, giving birth to their only son. Otha Lee had given the boy to his wife's sister to raise, but they had moved away, to Detroit, where more opportunities existed for black men during the Depression and World War 2. To Peggy's knowledge, Otha Lee had never heard from them again and had no idea how his son had grown up—not even whom he resembled.

All these rumors had come in drips and drabs from the house staff and occasionally from conversations Peggy had overheard between her father and Otha Lee. She had once seen her father place a brotherly hand on Otha Lee's shoulder when he shed tears while talking about his parents and wife and son.

Parking next to the house, Peggy got out and examined the overgrown cemetery, trying to picture it as it had been years ago when the congregation mowed the aisles to keep the weeds at bay, and the monuments shone in the sun after being scrubbed for Decoration Day by families that cared. Now it seemed the families had forgotten. Weeds thrived and trumpet vines covered many of the obelisks. Peggy picked her way through the rows, careful to avoid briars that scraped her ankles when she didn't pay attention to where she walked.

It's going to be beautiful here, and peaceful, she thought, visualizing the mown rows and colorful arrangements that would adorn each grave. Wondering about her own ancestors who might be buried here, she made a mental note to check the old church records to find out the names of any living descendants. She wanted to invite them to the homecoming she hoped Otha Lee would preach the day the church reopened for services.

Peggy had been lost in her daydream for so long that she failed to notice the man who had crept up behind her and was leaning against an ancient oak. So it startled her to turn and find herself staring into the steel-gray eyes of a man she had never seen before.

The man gazed at Peggy as if he had known every thought she had ever had. She was startled but then felt strangely calm, as if this stranger were someone she had been expecting for afternoon tea.

He was tall, taller than Peggy. He stood very straight, the tips of his fingers in his dungaree pockets, his plaid shirt untucked and flapping slightly in the late afternoon breeze.

"Sorry to sneak up on you, miss," he said, pulling a newspaper from his back pocket and unfolding it. "I'm looking for Peggy Nickles."

Peggy stepped from the cemetery, extending her hand. "I'm Peggy; and you are?"

"Joseph Davidson. I saw your ad for a handyman in the newspaper. Folks in town directed me here."

"Well, Mr. Davidson—"

"Joseph," he said, smiling nervously.

"Joseph. What are your qualifications?"

"Did a good bit of carpentry and woodworking. I spent some time up in Columbia doing that sort of thing."

"Do you have any references?" Peggy moved back a step into the shade. The late afternoon sun blinded her, and she could no longer make out the man's face.

"None around here. I can give you some names to contact up 'round the capital, but I don't know if they're still there. I worked with some pretty transient outfits." He glanced around the cemetery. "What is it you need doing?"

Peggy gestured toward the church. "I'm restoring this old church I bought."

Joseph placed his hands on his hips and surveyed the dilapidated building. "You bought a church?" He shook his head.

"Never heard of anybody doing that before. I thought God owned all the churches."

Peggy laughed. "God doesn't own buildings, only souls. Figuratively speaking, of course." She motioned to Joseph to follow her.

They cut through the cemetery toward the sanctuary's double doors. "This old graveyard could use a little resurrection itself," Joseph said. "No pun intended."

She smiled. "Maybe not intended but not offensive." Peggy pulled the keys from her dress pocket. Owning the church meant she did not have to climb through the window anymore, although sometimes she still did just for the fun of it. They stepped inside. A large garden spider had constructed an elaborate cobweb across the foyer since her last excursion.

"I'll get it," Joseph said. He grabbed a candlestick from the table and quickly knocked down the web. "Hope there ain't black widows in here. I knew a fellow got bit once. He didn't last three days."

"I don't know," Peggy said. "I guess we'll have to keep our eyes open, won't we?" She smiled and strolled up the center aisle, entranced as always by the cool blue glow cast by the faded windowpanes.

"What have you got in mind, Peggy?"

"For starters, the roof needs replacing, and parts of the floor, too. The entire building needs paint, inside and out. We must remove the old windows so someone can install the new ones."

"Those windows don't look too bad. Why not just replace the broken panes?"

"Because a church deserves stained glass."

Joseph whistled softly. "You're talking a pretty penny there. You might ought to get yourself a congregation and an offering before you start this."

Peggy sat in the minister's chair behind the pulpit. "You needn't worry about the money or the congregation. One already exists, and the Lord will provide the other."

"You seem pretty confident about that." He perched on the edge of the front pew. "You're talking about a lot of work here."

"Are you saying you'll take the job?"

Joseph paused, scratching his head. "You don't want to check me out first?"

Peggy was now standing in front of him, staring into his eyes. Joseph shifted his feet and backed away. "No need," she said. "I feel I can trust you."

"How's that?"

"You've listened to my plans and haven't told me I'm crazy, so you must be the man for the job."

They walked to Joseph's motorcycle.

"When do you want me to start?"

"Monday, 7:00 A.M. Bring your tools. I'll supply lunch and water. You'll be paid every Friday evening, and you won't be working alone."

"You mean somebody else thinks you're not crazy, too?" Joseph grinned and slung a leg over the cycle seat.

"I don't know whether he does or not," Peggy said, laughing softly. "He's a Negro, named Otha Lee Sturgis. You have any problems working with a colored man?"

"No, ma'am. I need this job. Long as it ain't Satan himself, I'll work with anybody." He jumped on the starter and revved the engine, causing Peggy to cover her ears.

She went back into the church and ran her hands across the ends of the pews as she walked up the aisle. She knelt at the splintery altar rail.

"Thank you, Lord," she prayed. "Thank you for this stranger, this angel you have sent. I put this church in your hands, to your glory, now and forever. Amen."

Locking the door, Peggy smiled at the twilight sun. Piece by piece her plan was coming together.

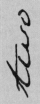

Otha Lee reared his chair onto its back legs. The elders were similarly situated around the back-yard, sipping colas and fanning gnats. It had been dry so far this summer—the yearly mosquito invasion usually didn't begin until July or August, and only then if it was wet and humid.

The elders met monthly at Otha Lee's or one of the elder's houses to discuss church business—not that there *was* much. With a congregation numbering only fifty strong, few topics merited serious discussion, so the meetings usually degenerated into gossip sessions.

Wycliffe Elkins stood and called the men to order. "This meeting of the Mount Gilead Missionary Baptist Church board of elders is now in session. Is there any old business to be dispensed with?" He surveyed the six men fanning gnats. None spoke.

"Is there any new business?"

Otha Lee cleared his throat and landed his chair with a thump.

"I have something to discuss, Brother Elkins." He stood and walked to the center of the group.

"Brother Otha Lee Sturgis has the floor. Or the yard, rather." Wycliffe grinned, settling back on a wicker rocking chair.

"Brothers, I have a miracle to announce. It is one I have dreamed of and prayed for my entire life, since my conversion on the night of fire."

A couple of the men rolled their eyes. Brother Otha Lee had a way of milking a story, and his tale of conversion had nearly reached biblical proportions. Otha Lee ignored the looks.

"Brothers, we are going to have ourselves a proper church building by the end of October."

He stood for a moment in the falling twilight, letting the announcement sink in.

"Otha Lee, I don't recall us starting any building fund or any stacks of money falling into the collection plate from the sky," said Wycliffe.

"That's right," Roy added. "Some do-gooder white church from up North give us some kind of grand donation or something?" Roy was much younger than the other elders. With an aging congregation, Otha Lee encouraged young people to aspire to leadership posts within the church. He found, however, that Roy could be a divisive force rather than a proponent of growth.

Otha Lee laughed. "No, son, this do-gooder came from our own backyard. Now you all know Miss Peggy Nickles."

"Yeah," said Roy. "Ain't she that crazy rich lady done bought the old Baptist church and graveyard?"

"One and the same. Although I don't appreciate you calling her crazy. She came by the house today and made me quite an offer."

"How's that, Otha Lee?" came a question from the shadows.

"She offered to deed over the church and rights to the burying ground if I—or we—help her fix up the building."

"She wants to sell us the church? Where we going to get that kind of money?" asked Wycliffe.

"Y'all are missing the point," Otha Lee said, putting his hands up to shush the loud whispering. "She is going to give, GIVE, us the church."

"Let me get this straight," said Roy. "She's going to let us use this white people's church and bury our Negro dead in the white people's church's white people's cemetery."

"That's right." Otha Lee looped his thumbs through his suspenders, beaming at the group.

"Like that's going to happen," said Roy, pulling out a rolling paper and a pouch of tobacco. "You got any idea what the white folks around here going to say about that? They ain't going to let that happen."

"Miss Peggy doesn't think it's a problem," Otha Lee said, sipping his soda.

"Miss Peggy, from what I understand, doesn't have any idea that she's even in this world with all us regular folk," said Roy. "Spent all her life being waited on hand and foot by servants—Negro servants. 'Til her daddy died and left her and her sisters with more money than God."

"Blasphemy, brother!" Otha Lee struggled to contain his voice. "Don't you all see? This is not about white or colored. It's about God answering a prayer. A prayer that I've prayed since, since—"

"Since your conversion by fire," the men bellowed in unison.

"You been drinking, Otha Lee?" Wycliffe placed a hand on his friend's shoulder. Otha Lee shrugged it away.

"Do you all want it or not?" Otha Lee shouted.

"It ain't a matter of us wanting it or not," Roy said, standing to face Otha Lee. "It's a matter of whether white folks gone let us have it."

"Miss Peggy is the only white folk we're dealing with here. She owns the church."

"She might own it, Brother Sturgis, but other folks own this county, and there ain't no way they are ever going to let Negroes worship in a white church or bury our dead in a white folks' cemetery." Roy pulled a last drag from his cigarette; the embers glowed briefly in the falling darkness. "Miss Peggy or no Miss Peggy, she wasn't thinking too straight when she made you that offer."

"Let's take a vote," Wycliffe said.

Otha Lee held up a hand. "No need for a vote. Miss Peggy made the offer to me personally. I have already decided I'm going to help her with the repairs."

"Then what's all this discussion been for?" Roy ground out the cigarette with his heel.

"Because I would like to have your help. Or at least your blessing."

Wycliffe rubbed his neck and looked away. "Any other business?"

Otha Lee looked around the circle, searching each face for some sign of agreement or support. He found none. Roy looked at Otha Lee, shrugged, and walked around the corner of the house, disappearing into the dusky dark and whistling an indecipherable tune.

"Meeting adjourned!" Wycliffe called after him.

Otha Lee looked around the group again and picked up the lantern he had lit in the middle of the circle.

"Will I be seeing you Sunday?" He wondered if he had convinced them he had gone crazy himself.

"Of course, Brother Sturgis, we'll be there." Wycliffe grasped his hand and shoulder, as did the others before filing into the night.

After everyone had gone, Otha Lee sat on the porch and hummed an old hymn, one his mother used to sing on nights when he was afraid of the dark. She taught him that light always followed the darkness, and he held that close in his heart when times got tough.

He stared up at the twinkling stars and prayed his prayer for a church, thanking God that even if everyone else thought he and Miss Peggy were crazy, he knew God did not, and that God alone could see it through.

Joseph loped up the outside staircase of the boardinghouse where he had taken a room earlier that day. He had just walked down the street to the general store, convincing the owner to stay open a few more minutes so he could pick up some much-needed essentials to last through the next few days. Joseph wanted to make sure he didn't waste all his money before he received his first week's pay.

Setting the brown paper sacks on the small green wooden table that would act as his dining room suite, he took out a bag of pork rinds, a box of soda crackers, some cans of pork and beans and tomato soup, and put them in the small cupboard. The room came with a small refrigerator and a hot plate. Joseph had worked for a few weeks as a short-order cook, so he knew enough bachelor cooking to survive. He placed a pound of bacon, some eggs, and a quart of milk in the refrigerator. He found the bag of grits at the bottom of the bag and set it on the shelf next to the other provisions.

The bare lightbulb cast a harsh light on the room, and Joseph thought he might buy a small lamp to add a little ambience to the place. Having just spent twenty years in a very bad atmosphere, he felt a great need for creature comforts. In fact, this was not the first boardinghouse he had visited. An old man who cared little about providing anything other than beds for his renters ran the first. Left with little himself, it seemed the old man, in his state of grief and denial over losing his wife, found no need to provide comfort—physical or emotional—to anyone else. After a quick look around, Joseph decided he could do better and had come upon this place.

While wandering around town that day, Joseph had enjoyed watching people taking care of their yards: mowing lawns, planting vegetable gardens, or just cutting early summer flowers for what he imagined were special family dinners on screened porches. It had been a while since he had spent any appreciable time breathing fresh air, and his body couldn't get enough of walking. He considered the motorcycle more of a practicality than a necessity, finding it a faster mode of transportation than shoe leather.

It was strange being so close to home, yet feeling like he was still locked away. He wondered if he would ever go back, if the folks there would ever take him back. No one ever wanted to hear that it had been an accident, an awful accident he had tried to stop even as it was happening.

He shook his head—he could not think about that now, would not think about it. He was free now, with a chance for a brand-new start.

Lounging against the headboard, Joseph chewed thoughtfully on a fried pork rind, its saltiness twanging in his cheeks.

It tasted better than anything he had eaten in years. He concluded freedom could change the taste of food just the same as it changed a person's outlook on life.

Miss Peggy—that was how everyone in town referred to his new boss. Nobody called her just plain Peggy. He gathered that she was quite wealthy and, like many people say when speaking of the wealthy, eccentric. Funny, he thought, if you're poor and you act a little strange, people call you nuts or looney. But give a person a little cash, a big house, and a fancy car, and everyone automatically forgives you for acting strange and graces you with the title of eccentricity. "That eccentric Peggy Nickles," he had heard her called down at the diner.

She had looked mysterious, standing there in the dying sun in that overgrown graveyard. Almost as if she expected an angel to greet her. Joseph had had some close encounters with the other side of life, as the song put it, and he was now placing his energies on staying on its right side; hopefully, when he closed his eyes for the last time, he would be seeing the pearly gates instead of the red-hot tines of a pitchfork.

The church looked like a monumental project for two men, and Joseph hoped this Otha Lee Peggy had talked about was up to the challenge. Joseph had worked a few odd jobs on his way out of the capital, picking up enough cash to buy his ride. The motorcycle wasn't much to look at, but it was serviceable, a bargain buy from a Fort Jackson soldier on his way overseas to Korea. Maybe working this church job would give him enough cash to get his own place—nothing with a church or graveyard, of course—but a little trailer house, something he could set up on a country acre. Something he could, for the first time in his life, call his own.

Sunday afternoon, Peggy sat on the front porch painting her toenails a fire-engine red, when Roxie drove up, honking the horn, "Shake, Rattle, 'n Roll" blasting from the radio.

Peggy put her feet down and sighed. She and Roxie, who was twice married and twice divorced, had been friends since grammar school. The first husband, shell-shocked from the war, drank so much that he could barely earn a living, and what living he did earn he managed to pour down his throat before Roxie could get hold of it to pay the bills. Husband Number Two drank AND smacked Roxie around. Once she had arrived at Peggy's doorstep at 2:00 A.M., bleeding all over her white blouse from a gash beneath her eye, caused by a right-handed uppercut augmented by a garish Masonic ring.

Having decided enough was enough, Roxie scraped together enough money to attend beauty school and worked in a small salon downtown giving blue rinses and permanent waves to the town matriarchs. When she wasn't working, she spent the bulk of her time running back and forth from the beach to the mountains or the lake or anywhere else that wasn't Bonham.

"Peggs!" she called, using her friend's childhood nickname.

"Hey, Roxie." Peggy pulled a rocking chair from the wall. "If you want something to drink, you'll have to fix it yourself." She wiggled her toes in the air.

"Not thirsty." Roxie bounced across the porch, tossing her purse onto the porch swing, setting it swaying. "Come with me to Cape Hatteras."

"What's in Cape Hatteras?" Peggy was accustomed to these impromptu invitations.

"I don't know. A lighthouse? Other than that, I'm not sure. That's why we're going—to find out." Roxie pulled out a nail file and began manicuring Peggy's fingernails. "I have the entire week off from the salon and I'm hitting the road."

"So what else is new?" Peggy smiled and watched as her friend bent to her work. Their friendship had always mystified Peggy's family. Roxie was outgoing, the class clown, always ready for fun and adventure. Peggy had always been more settled, cerebral, quiet, more prone to reading a good book or sketching a peaceful landscape than tearing up the dance floor.

"So you want to go?" Roxie sat back, splaying Peggy's fingers to appraise her progress.

"I can't. We're starting work on the church this week."

Roxie rolled her eyes. "Peggy, why in the world don't you just sell that old thing? That graveyard gives me the creeps. Thinking about all those old dead bodies rotting up and fertilizing the weeds? No thank you, ma'am."

"I like the idea," said Peggy, watching the graveyard as if at any moment a weed might take a sudden growth spurt. "Life recirculating. Old life creating new life." She stood at the porch banister and surveyed the stones standing like broken teeth.

"Who is we?"

"What?" Peggy turned to face her friend.

"We. You said 'we're' starting work."

"Oh. Otha Lee, for one."

"You didn't." Roxie gave her a sly grin. She had been the first to know of Peggy's plans for the church. "You said for one. Who's two?"

"I most certainly did—I told you I would. And for two, a man named Joseph Davidson."

Roxie tapped her chin. "Never heard of him."

"I don't believe he's from around here. He just showed up out of the blue looking for work. I needed a helper for Otha Lee, so I hired him."

"Just like that. A total stranger." Roxie went into a trance before collapsing into one of her paroxysms of ecstasy, as Peggy often referred to them. "How romantic!" Two bad marriages hadn't dampened Roxie's views on love, marriage, or her own or Peggy's likely prospects for eternal bliss.

"I swear, sometimes you act more like fifteen than thirty-five," Peggy said, suppressing a smile. "Romance has nothing to do with it. I needed someone with a strong back, and he looked like he had one."

Roxie leaned forward. "And what else did he have?" Her eyes twinkled as she rubbed her palms together.

Peggy glared at Roxie impatiently. "Nothing you would be interested in."

"Hmmm. Must be more than you're admitting."

Peggy thought back. All she really remembered about Joseph were those steel-gray eyes. Eyes that were not cold, in spite of their color, but held a sparkle, like sunlight on shimmering water.

Rarely did Peggy look at men anymore. It wasn't lack of interest or that she did not want to be married; she hadn't given up on the idea completely. She had merely given up hope. Her disappointments had been many and severe, and she felt that her heart could no longer take the abuse.

A few of her suitors had not been all bad. Attractive enough. Clean enough. Genial enough. Boring enough that when she arrived home from dates she literally burst into tears from having spent entire evenings with a smile pasted on her face concealing her sheer dread of having to explain another joke or give a lesson on the latest literary masterpiece or political event. None of these men was a challenge. They lacked motivation and curiosity; they were interested in little more than what they had to do at work tomorrow and how soon they might get their next raise.

Roxie returned to the present concern. "So, are you coming or not? I'm ready to hit the road."

"Like I said, we're starting work tomorrow."

"You mean they're starting work. I can just see you swinging a hammer and toting two-by-fours."

"You never know." Peggy smiled and hugged Roxie. "Have a good trip and try to behave."

"*Try* being the operative word?" Roxie pulled back with a mischievous expression. She skipped down the steps, swinging her purse wildly, and jumped into the car. "Say hey to the carpenter for me," she hollered, then drove off.

Peggy gazed at the church, picturing it whole again—the splendor of the new windows and a crowd of people ascending the steps for the first service in the refurbished sanctuary. She prayed for her vision to come true and that the work of Otha Lee and Joseph's hands would make it so.

"Aunt Peggy?"

Peggy jumped, then turned to find a slight, blond-headed child leaning her bicycle against the front steps.

"Gail!" Mindless of her toenails, Peggy ran down the steps and wrapped her arms around her favorite niece. In fact, Gail was her only niece, but Peggy thought that even if she had others, Gail would always be the favorite. "I can't believe you rode your bicycle all this way. Your mother must have pitched a fit."

"She don't know I'm here."

"Doesn't know you're here," Peggy corrected. Gail regularly reverted to the local vernacular whenever she came back from boarding school, trying to fit in with her public school-educated friends. Peggy wondered if she should call Eva to let her know her daughter's whereabouts. Not that Eva would care. She was always shipping Gail off to boarding schools and summer camps. "Let me guess—she's sending you off to camp again."

Gail nodded solemnly. "I was hoping I could come stay with you, Aunt Peggy. You know, for the summer."

Peggy took Gail's hand and led her to the porch swing where they sat listening to the summer breeze rustle through the oak, sycamore, and maple trees that filled the front yard. At twelve, Gail was still a little girl in spirit but had begun showing signs of a young woman in her physical aspects. Although the child appeared fragile, Peggy knew that she possessed great strength and a vibrant soul that somehow helped her through her mother's seeming indifference and her father's incapacity for affection. Peggy felt drawn to fill the gaps.

"Honey, you know I would love for you to stay with me. Given the state of my relationship with your mother, though, I don't think she would allow it. In fact, I already tried to talk to her, but she didn't seem too inclined to let you come."

Gail turned an innocent face to Peggy. "Why don't you and Mother get along?"

Peggy wondered that herself. Eva was thirteen years older than Peggy, so they hadn't really grown up together. As a child, Eva treated her youngest sister as more of an annoyance than a sibling. In adulthood, Peggy had tired of Eva's constant bossiness, her need to dictate terms to everyone in the family concerning their finances, their homes, and their personal lives. Ironic that Eva was right: Peggy *was* showing a rebellious streak by buying the church. Even while signing the papers, she had experienced a passing flash that Eva would completely overreact to her choice of how she wanted to spend her inheritance.

Peggy became aware of a hand being waved in front of her face.

"You in there, Aunt Peggy?"

"I'm here, Gail." She turned to face her niece. "When are you supposed to leave?"

"Next Saturday."

"We're not having another brunch until a week from Wednesday. I guess I'll have to call her." She pulled her niece close. "I can't make you any promises."

"I know." They swung quietly for several minutes until Gail pulled away. "When I come to stay with you, can I help you work on the church?"

Peggy brightened. "Sure you can. I might even put you to digging around in that spooky old graveyard."

Gail wrinkled her nose. "What if I accidentally dig up a dead person? What if their spirits get loose? Then we'll have ghosts running all over the church!"

Peggy had to laugh. "You mean like old Jacob Marley in *A Christmas Carol*? Doomed to carry his heavy chains of greed and avarice?"

"Exactly." Gail looked worried.

"Gail, that story was just about a dream of old Ebenezer Scrooge, remember? It's what they call a cautionary tale, reminding us how we ought to live. So to answer your question, if we dig up a dead person, we'll just bury them back and everything will be fine." Peggy grabbed Gail and buried her in a hug. "Enough spooky stuff on this beautiful day. Why don't I get my bike and we'll ride down to the river?"

"Great."

Peggy went inside to don her tennis shoes, then to the old shed out back where she rolled out her dusty bicycle. She found Gail sitting on hers when she came around the corner of the house.

"Ready?" Peggy said, gliding away toward the Lowland River.

"Always," Gail replied, racing to catch up.

Pedaling rapidly, Peggy was glad she had not taken Roxie up on her offer. A lazy Sunday afternoon bike ride with a curious twelve-year-old beat a day at the beach any way you looked at it.

three

The sun rose behind the thicket of tall, spindly pines that bordered the church on two sides. A pair of cardinals flew back and forth, low to the ground, bringing breakfast to their tiny, hidden nestlings.

Otha Lee stood before the church, breathing in the strong, sweet scent of pale yellow honeysuckle veiling the outside walls. The morning was cool, but the heat would come on hard and fast around 11:00. He had come prepared with old towels to use for sweat rags and a battered tool kit. Turning, he spotted a man approaching on a motorcycle. Dismounting, the man walked tall and purposefully, as if he were planning to walk all the way to the Pacific Ocean, not just to some falling down church on a Butler County back road.

"Can I help you, sir?" Otha Lee said.

"Peggy hired me to help work on the church building." The stranger tipped his hat and extended his hand. "Joseph Davidson."

Otha Lee took the proffered hand. He could feel the calloused palm. "Name's Otha Lee Sturgis. You can call me Otha Lee."

"Otha Lee." Joseph shook his hand, noting its firm grip, one Otha Lee polished on many a witness night and Sunday morning greeting. "Peggy told me I'd be working with you. Asked me if I had any objections to working with a Negro."

"What did you tell her?" Otha Lee asked, placing his toolbox on the church steps.

"Told her it didn't matter. I need the work. Man, I'd work with you if you were purple with green hair."

Otha Lee laughed. "Time we spend the summer out here in this hot sun, we both might turn purple."

Joseph surveyed the overgrown chapel. Besides the honeysuckle, trumpet vines and other unidentifiable foliage enveloped the wooden walls. Missing windowpanes gave the impression that if the building had been human, its eyes would have been knocked out. Jagged holes scarred the roof, and the front steps tilted at odd angles, an accident waiting to happen. "Quite a job waiting for us, ain't it?"

"Yeah. But I been waiting for this my whole life, and I'm up to it. Are you?"

"Sure. I got the impression you're in charge, so where do you want me to start?"

Otha Lee smiled into the distance, pushing his straw hat back on his head. "Son, there's your boss right there." He gestured toward the house, where Peggy emerged wearing sky-blue pedal pushers, a sleeveless calico blouse, and a bright blue bandanna in her hair.

"Gentlemen, I see you've met," she called, picking her way through the graveyard. The men took off their hats and waited for her arrival before putting them back on.

"We were just wondering where you want us to start," Joseph said.

"First things first. We're starting work on a house of the Lord here, so I think it is only appropriate that we start by putting it all in his hands."

Joseph shifted a little, looking down at his feet.

"Something wrong, Mr. Davidson?" Peggy leaned her head down to catch his eyes.

"No, ma'am, and please, call me Joseph." He let out a deep breath. "It's just been a while since I did any praying."

"That's okay. Otha Lee will take care of it. He's a preacher."

Joseph snatched off his hat again. "I'm sorry, Reverend, I didn't know."

Otha Lee held up his hands. "I'm just a man like you, no need for formalities. Now, shall we pray?" The three bowed their heads. "Dear Lord, as we begin the work on your house of worship, we ask that you guide our hands as they saw and hammer and paint, our eyes as we look for what needs doing, our bodies when they become tired and weary, and our hearts as we seek to serve you by restoring this mess of wood to new glory. We thank you for this chance to bring honor and glory to your name and to your work and your words, heavenly Father. We ask these blessings in the name of your son, Jesus Christ. Amen."

"Amen," said Peggy.

Joseph amened silently.

Peggy reached into her pocket and withdrew two keys. "I had one of these made for each of you. They are the keys to the front door of the sanctuary. That way you won't have to wait on me to open the door every morning. Or in case I'm not here."

Joseph stared at the key in his palm. No one had ever trusted him with the key to anything other than wherever he happened to be living. Otha Lee took his and smiled at Peggy. She nodded toward the door.

Otha Lee marched up the wobbly steps, holding the key in front of him like a golden chalice before he carefully placed it in the lock, feeling the tumblers click as he turned it. He pushed into the swirling dust falling in the pale blue morning light.

"Hallelujah and praise God!" he shouted.

Peggy and Joseph followed him in, standing apart, surveying the damaged sanctuary.

"Where do we start?" Joseph picked up an overturned pew and began hauling it toward the back of the building.

Peggy realized she had given little thought to what should be done first. After all, she was not a carpenter—she had no idea in what order construction should take place. Otha Lee noticed her contorted expression.

"I suggest we begin with the roof."

"Okay," Peggy said, looking up at the sagging rafters and holes that peeked through the shingles. "Tell me what you need, and I'll go get it."

Otha Lee laughed. "Miss Peggy, I don't think you going to be fitting any roofing shingles in the backseat of that flying phantom you got out there. Joseph had best take my truck and get the supplies. Come here, son, and we'll make a list of materials."

Joseph sat down next to Otha Lee. Peggy walked back to the house to call the hardware store and arrange for credit. Meanwhile, Joseph glanced around at the dust-covered furnishings.

"She's really serious about this, ain't she?"

Otha Lee licked the end of his pencil and scribbled some items on the back of an old church bulletin. "Joseph, she is one determined young lady, and I am one determined old man."

"What is it with her? She got more money than sense?"

"Some might say that, but I don't think so. I think Miss Peggy's looking for something."

"Like what?" Joseph laid his arm on the back of the pew and shifted to face the old man.

"Something she's lost. Maybe something she never had. Maybe she's just trying to stand out amongst all them bossy sisters of hers. Those girls are like their mama—set on perfection and unused to anyone rocking the boat."

"Is that what Peggy's doing?"

"You could say that. It's possible she's about to cause a shipwreck." Otha Lee stuck the pencil over his right ear. "Reckon she's depending on us to make the ship sail."

Peggy slammed down the telephone receiver. She couldn't believe what had just happened. She had called Grosvenor's Hardware Store to arrange credit. Mr. Grosvenor himself had answered the call.

"Now, Miss Nickles, you know me and your daddy had a good working relationship and all, and I know Otha Lee personally, but I can't go around giving Negroes credit."

"For one thing, Mr. Grosvenor, I'm not asking credit for Otha Lee, I'm asking credit for myself. I'll be the one paying the bills. For another, even if it was Otha Lee asking for credit, I don't see how in the world you could refuse just because he's colored. That's not fair; it's not right, and you know it."

A sigh percolated through the lines. "Miss Nickles, they're bad pay, slow pay, and no pay. You can't trust 'em. I'd advise you to get someone else to take over that there church. It could lead to problems."

It already has, Peggy mused. "As I have told other objectors to this project, it is none of your business what I plan to do here."

"I'm sorry, but I just can't give you credit."

"Well then, Mr. Grosvenor, I'll just take my business elsewhere."

She looked out the window and drew a deep breath. She had to calm down before going back. Her sisters' resistance she could understand, but a merchant missing an opportunity to sell a truckload, probably several truckloads, of building supplies—it just didn't wash.

Otha Lee and Joseph were standing in front of the church, watching her house. Peggy checked her face in the mirror and decided Otha Lee didn't have to know what had just happened. She hoped her expression wouldn't betray it.

Joseph shook his head. His questions to Otha Lee were only leading to other questions. Peggy returned in a huff.

"Something wrong, Miss Peggy?"

"No. Not the worst problem, anyway. The hardware store refused to give me credit." She lifted her chin and smiled thinly. "I guess the Nickles name doesn't count for as much as I thought it did."

"So what are you going to do?" Joseph took the list Otha Lee was holding out to him.

"Pay cash, of course." Joseph tried not to stare as Peggy fumbled and finally pulled several bills from her pocket. "This should cover what we need for now, shouldn't it?" She offered the money to Joseph, who only nodded and folded it, placing it carefully in his dungaree pocket.

"Keys are in the truck," said Otha Lee. "I'll tell you how to get to Grosvenor's."

"No." Peggy spoke sharply, then looked at the ground. "We'll be using Stubbs' Feed and Dry Goods instead."

Otha Lee pushed back his hat. "They cost more, Miss Peggy."

"I know. It's not a problem."

Otha Lee shrugged and Joseph got in the old Ford truck, which hesitated on the first couple of hits at the starter but finally caught. He gunned the engine a couple of times before turning it around and heading back toward town.

Peggy watched him leave. "What do you think, Otha Lee? Will he be much help?"

"Hard to tell. I ain't seen him swing a hammer yet, but his hands are calloused. That's a good sign."

Peggy studied Otha Lee. His graying hair made his almond skin seem sallow. "Was I wrong to ask you to do this?" Her eyes wandered over his swollen knuckles, and she had noticed that his limp was more pronounced. "Are you sure you're up to it? I can get somebody else to do the work."

Otha Lee met her gaze. "Miss Peggy, your offer was a gift from God. Saying no to that would be like saying no to the deity himself." He walked to the pulpit and spread his hands in the air. "This is the day the Lord hath made. Rejoice and be glad in it," he exclaimed. "Miss Peggy, you go on back to the house. Joseph will bring you the change at lunch. I'll be sure he don't skim none of it."

Peggy walked to the door before making a small half turn. "I was just making sure."

"Of me, Miss Peggy? Or yourself?"

Peggy stepped onto the tree-shaded back porch and sat on an old wicker chair. Otha Lee's last question had struck a chord. She knew many people in Bonham believed she was peculiar for buying the church. Just a ditzy rich girl trying to find something to do with her time and all that Nickles money.

The money. She knew that in her own misguided way that was what she was trying to relinquish. Peggy wanted to be a normal person. Not a poor person. She had never been poor, but she knew the poor had a much different way of life. Both having money and not having it created conflicts unique to each corresponding situation. It had never been Peggy's desire to be deprived in any way. She was well aware that her parents had spoiled her, and it was obvious to everyone that she liked her luxuries. The new convertible was evidence of that.

Hers was a different kind of poverty. A poverty of the heart and soul. She felt lonesome, even among her friends, where the shallow conversations and constant emphasis on possessions bored her. Even her sisters fixated on their own desires for expensive clothes, lavish houses, modern furniture, and socially acceptable husbands. Her sisters were cookie-cutter versions of their parents and even their grandparents. It was as if it were all genetic that men pursued certain professions and women embraced the compulsory avocations. It was a certain way of life each was born to, like the tradition where the daughter wears her mother's wedding dress. Only the dress had become shabby—the lace rotten, the buttons falling off, the entire garment in danger of falling to the floor, exposing the betrothed's ratty undergarments for the entire assembly's perusal, comment, and subsequent gossip. Excepting Gail, Peggy felt her family was cursed to live a life of style rather than substance and that someday all their epitaphs might read "They wore it well."

It was Peggy's time to break away. Each time she saw her sisters, she knew they did not take her plans for the church seriously. They viewed it as a short-lived hobby, one she would quickly grow tired of and dispose of as she had so many eligible suitors since the war.

Nevertheless, Peggy relished the dream of bringing the church to a new glory, even if she did not plan to use it herself. She knew Otha Lee would allow her to attend the church if she wished, but she knew it would not be hers anymore, that it would belong to Otha Lee and his congregation.

She watched Otha Lee walk around the church, sizing up its defects, knowing that he had his own vision of how it might look, primed and painted, gleaming white on a sunny Sunday morning as his flock entered dressed in their pressed suits, starched dresses, and stylish hats.

Glancing at her watch, Peggy thought she should get started on lunch. Cooking was another talent she had been forced to acquire since she had moved into the manse, having grown tired of the trek between Belva's and Beatrice's and Eva's homes for her evening suppers and Sabbath dinners. Priscilla, her mother's cook, had shown her many secrets of the dishes she prepared for the Nickles throughout her forty years in the family's employ.

Now Peggy surveyed the pantry and panicked. She had cooked for herself and her sisters and knew what they liked.

But what in the world do you cook for two men rebuilding a church?

Otha Lee eased from the truck and held on to the banister, feeling his way up the steps. He could not remember when he had been so tired or so sore. His body, while getting old, had also become unaccustomed to the hard work that had been his entire life as a young man. It had been years since he had put in such a hard day.

Yet the hurt felt good. It was for a purpose, a higher calling. Otha Lee believed in his heart that the Lord would give him the strength and stamina to see the church restoration completed.

Joseph proved a good helper, more familiar with construction techniques than Otha Lee. The younger man confidently ran up and down the ladder all day, pulling off shingles, and back and forth to the truck and the hardware store, loading and unloading supplies. Their first day had gone slowly, what with only the two of them working, but it had gone well. Otha Lee found the younger man quiet but dedicated, with a laid-back style and an easy sense of humor.

Otha Lee flopped into the rocking chair. The late afternoon heat and humidity had been too much for both men, and they agreed with Peggy that 4:00 would be a good knocking-off time. They would also have the weekends for rest and restoration.

He saw now that it would take several months to accomplish their task. Closely inspecting the structure, they had found termite damage, a constant hazard in the hot, humid coastal plain. Miss Peggy had not been pleased to hear it but promised that funds were available for the unexpected repairs.

Otha Lee gathered enough strength to make it into the house where he turned on the oscillating fan as he passed. He laid down on the bed, spread-eagled, too tired to change out of his sweaty clothing. He stared at the picture of Jesus that hung on the wall across from the foot of his bed, where it would be the first thing he saw when he awoke each morning and the last thing before he fell asleep each night.

"Dear Lord, give me strength," he began to pray, falling asleep before he could finish his request.

Joseph strolled down Bonham's main street, window-shopping and nodding amiably at the people he passed. It had been a great day. His muscles felt good, stretched and taut, back in action; he loved the feel of work, had never shied away from it. He carried a small bag of peaches he had purchased from an itinerant produce seller on the outskirts of town. Feeling inside the bag, he brought one out and bit into it, catching the juice that ran down his chin with the side of his hand. The fruit was cool and sweet, the way his life felt now. Although he was alone, he felt companionable, as if everyone was his friend.

Sitting on a park bench beneath a sprawling elm, Joseph pondered his new employer and the old Negro preacher. In his limited experience, he had never met anyone as trusting as Peggy Nickles. She was completely guileless, seemingly unafraid of anyone, although Joseph sensed she was the kind of person who held close counsel on whatever might be bothering her. Much like himself.

Otha Lee, however, was another story. Joseph sensed the old man trusted him, but only within eyeshot, at least for the moment. He seemed a good man. Joseph overheard him breaking into spirituals and belting out Bible verses from time to time as if Joseph weren't even around and he was simply preaching to the birds that nested in the nearby woods. Joseph had never been much on going to church, but he had no objections to those who did. Peggy's announcement that Otha Lee was an ordained man of God and a messenger of the Lord and Savior had come as no real surprise. Otha Lee had not asked about Joseph's beliefs or religious background, for which Joseph was relieved. That aspect of his life became complicated early, and Joseph did not want to lie to the preacher.

Two young girls, all of sixteen, came down the sidewalk, looking at Joseph and giggling. Joseph grinned and giggled back, casting an admiring glance at their bare legs as they passed. Joseph wasn't looking to get involved with any women yet, especially minors, but he wasn't opposed to a little overt flirtation. He had missed a lot in the last twenty years, especially women. Sure, he'd had a few girlfriends once upon a time, but that was what it was—a long-ago fairy tale, but one that had an unhappy ending.

Joseph's gaze drifted up and down the street. He nodded as he finished the peach and pitched the remains into a nearby trash can. *This is right,* he thought. *It's good.*

Maybe now he had a place where he could make a new beginning. Maybe, finally, a place he could call home.

Four

Peggy pulled her convertible into Eva's driveway. Belva and Beatrice had apparently arrived together; Belva's burgundy Studebaker was parked in the circular drive. The gardener, Ezekiel, was trimming the boxwoods as if he were cutting hair, clipping short lengths, then running his fingers over the same area, feeling for long straggles.

"Good morning, Zeke," Peggy called.

"Morning, Miss Peggy. Fine day, ain't it?" He smiled, smoothing his palm over the shrub.

"Yes, it is."

Peggy let herself in the front door. Eva preferred that everyone, including her sisters, ring the doorbell so her white-gloved butler could show them into the parlor. Being family, Peggy saw no reason to stand on ceremony.

Belva, Beatrice, and Eva sat in the back parlor; Peggy could hear them as she walked down the hall. She stopped to admire a photograph of Gail, now away at camp over Peggy's objections. Eva had adamantly refused to allow Gail to spend the summer with Peggy. When Peggy made the dreaded phone call, she knew by Eva's tone it was useless.

"You know if it was just you, and you were living in town where Gail would be exposed to more cultural activities, I wouldn't object to her spending an afternoon or two with you," Eva had said, with an edge of insincerity. A tone that meant she felt any time Gail spent with Peggy would be wasted.

"If I promise not to let her work in the cemetery—"

"Oh, dear sister, she's not getting anywhere near that old cemetery. Snakes and what-all else might be crawling around in there. Much less a Negro preaching who-knows-what and an itinerant carpenter from, from—who-knows-where?" Her voice rose.

"I assure you that Otha Lee and Joseph are no threat to her. I'll be with her all the time."

"This is useless, Peggy, as usual. She's going to camp. It will do a lot more for her social standing than spending the summer watching you pull weeds in an old tumbledown cemetery." She was silent for a moment. "I'll see you at brunch," she said precisely and had hung up before Peggy could voice another objection.

Peggy carefully replaced the photo when she heard her name mentioned. Eva was obviously in the thralls of a captive audience.

"I drove past that old church the other day. Place would be better off bulldozed than resurrected. She is going to fritter away her entire trust fund on that albatross and wind up asking us for help. I can feel it coming."

Peggy crept down the hall, staying on the Persian rugs, out of sight of the parlor's wide pocket-door opening. She heard the twins sighing in unison.

"You know she always has had peculiar ideas," Belva said.

"It's just one of her notions," Beatrice added. "She'll grow tired of it soon, and that whole place will have a For Sale sign on it. Just bide your time, Eva."

"I'm not so sure about that." Peggy caught sight of her oldest sister in a gilt-edged mirror. "You should have seen the piles of building materials she's had hauled out there. You'd think she was building a grand cathedral on the finest paved street in Rome. I tell you, she's sparing no expense."

Peggy padded back to the grand front parlor, a room usually reserved for guests. Eva's husband, along with Belva's and Beatrice's, now ran the Nickles Textile Company. Their father had built the company into a major force during the war, garnering numerous defense contracts, and afterward had managed to corner a market in the New York-based fashion industry. Their father's frugality and shrewd business acumen had made them all rich, set for life. The company continued to generate income and dividends from which the entire family drew, as stipulated in their father's will.

Sitting on an antique Duncan Phyfe sofa, Peggy enjoyed the cool breeze blowing through the open windows. She drank in the scent of freshly mown grass mixed with that of the pink roses arranged in a vase before her. In Eva's one acquiescence to family heritage, large daguerreotypes of their grandparents graced the wall over the mantel, their faces staring sternly from the past. Peggy began to feel as if the past was reproaching her as well as the present. Lately, Peggy had become the almost complete focus of her sisters' attentions at these family gatherings. It dawned on her that perhaps her sisters had too little to occupy their time and minds, and thus had latched onto Peggy's obsessions as a focus for their energies.

She debated whether to announce her presence. If she left, she would never hear the end of it. An unspoken rule stated that no one was allowed to miss a Wednesday brunch unless the family physician certified them as being on their deathbed. She briefly wondered if she could bribe Dr. Jasper into faking a death certificate.

More than a week had passed since Otha Lee and Joseph had begun work on the church. Peggy was frustrated at the slow progress but knew she had to make allowances for age in Otha Lee's case and the rising summer heat for both men. Yet they needed to work fast to make the roof repairs to protect the church interior from further damage.

Each day, the men came to the screened back porch, where Peggy had set up a picnic table and a box fan so the men could eat quietly and cool themselves. Cooking for them gave her a chance to expand her recipe repertoire. She hadn't had any complaints, but she had noticed some amused glances exchanged between Otha Lee and Joseph. She carefully noted which dishes these looks followed so she would know not to cook them again or whether the recipe might need adjustment.

"Where in the world could she be?" Eva marched down the hall and pulled up short when she noticed Peggy with her nose pressed against the rose blossoms. "Why are you hiding in here? Didn't you ring the bell?"

She had missed her chance for escape.

"The breeze felt so pleasant coming through the window, I thought I would just sit here and enjoy it."

"You could have at least let us know you were here."

"You seemed to be doing fine without me."

Eva looked at Belva and Beatrice, who stood behind her like two yellow chicks in matching dresses. "Well, honey, just what did you hear?"

"Enough." Peggy picked up her purse and headed toward the door. Belva and Beatrice moved to block her.

"Now what you heard, Peggy, why, we're just concerned about you, that's all," said Belva.

"You know we don't wish anything ill on your little project," added Beatrice.

"That's exactly what I mean." Peggy threw her purse across the room where it popped open, its contents skittering across the floor. "Has there ever been any time in my life when any of you have taken me seriously? When you haven't considered everything I have ever done or tried to do just 'another of Peggy's little projects,' another of 'Peggy's whims'?"

"Calm down, honey." Eva tried to put her hand on Peggy's shoulder.

"Don't touch me." Peggy stepped back and straightened her skirt. "Believe it or not, what I'm doing at the church is important. It may not mean much in your country-club, garden-club, Junior-League world, but it means something to me." She paused and rubbed her forehead. "It means something to Otha Lee. It might just mean something to God."

"To God?" said Beatrice.

"Since when did you become so religious?" asked Eva.

Peggy sighed. She wondered if it would be worth the effort. Her attendance at church had been scanty at best in recent years. There was something about a sermon that caused her mind to wander, and she usually discovered at the end that she had no idea what the minister's message had been. What good was it to go to church, only to miss the point of going?

"You know," she said, gathering up her scattered belongings, "I don't care what any of you think. It's none of your business anyway. Just as what any of you do with your trust funds is no business of mine."

The sisters followed Peggy to the front door.

"Please, dear, come back and have some lunch," said Belva. "I think your sugar might be low."

"Sugar, my foot," Peggy muttered, as the screen door creaked shut behind her.

Otha Lee and Joseph sat on a couple of crumbling gravestones, eating the peanut butter sandwiches Peggy had left for them on the back porch table.

"Where did Peggy disappear to this morning all primped up?" Joseph took a big bite, chewing close to half the sandwich at once.

Otha Lee chuckled. "You ain't met Miss Peggy's sisters, have you?"

"No, sir. I ain't met much of anybody since I came to town."

"Miss Peggy's sisters have a lunch set up so's they can stay in touch now that their mama and papa's done passed."

"Oh. I didn't know her parents were gone." He chewed thoughtfully. "I did notice she referred to them in the past tense. Reckon that should've told me something. Anyway, she didn't seem too happy—I hope she ain't going to be ill with us when she comes back."

"If you ever get to meet Misses Belva and Beatrice and Eva, you'll know why she gets that way." Otha Lee finished his sandwich and polished an apple against his shirt. "Three peas in a pod. Peggy's the odd gal out of that bunch."

"How so?"

"Speaks her mind. Don't cotton to joining onto something just because everybody else is joining."

"Explains a lot." Joseph wiped his mouth on his sleeve.

Joseph had taken to studying Peggy on a regular basis. He liked learning new things, particularly new women, probably because he hadn't had that opportunity in a while.

He had never seen a woman try so hard to be good at men's things and women's things all at once. Probably because she was single and lived alone, he reasoned. He also wondered why, in spite of her wealth, she didn't hire more help, both for herself and the church repairs.

One afternoon, Peggy surprised Joseph when she announced that she was tired of watching them have all the fun and that she intended to come out first thing the next morning so they could teach her how to carpenter. Otha Lee had broken into hysterical laughter after she went back inside. Joseph supposed it was because he thought the lady was joking. It turned out she wasn't.

At 8:00 sharp the next morning, Peggy had emerged from the house wearing dungarees and a blue work shirt, a bandanna tied around her neck, shod in a brand-new pair of miniature brogans. She demanded they send her up the ladder with a crossbeam, but Otha Lee had gently steered her toward pulling nails from the rotten floor.

He had to hand it to Otha Lee. The old man knew how to handle her. At first, Joseph felt uncomfortable, like Peggy was constantly watching him. As the days went by, he soon found himself showing her how to do things, pointing her to the right tool or showing her a safer or faster way to accomplish a task. He still felt watched, but as he was studying her, he began to realize that Peggy was studying him, too.

A cloud of dust down the road caught their attention. "Miss Peggy," said Otha Lee, slapping bread crumbs from his chest and lap. He rose from the tombstone, tipping his hat as her car roared by.

"She ain't been gone long," Joseph said. "Reckon something's wrong?"

"Judging from the way she came down that road, I'd guess it is."

Peggy slammed the car door and caught sight of Otha Lee and Joseph.

"I am not paying y'all to stand around staring at me. Get back to work." She stomped up the front steps, slamming the door behind her so quickly she caught the hem of her dress in it.

"The general has spoken." Otha Lee arranged his hat, picked up his hammer, and hustled toward the church.

Joseph stared at the house. He decided he might have to go back to school and take some extra coursework to figure out the uneven behavior of that eccentric Miss Peggy Nickles.

Peggy took several deep breaths, trying to calm herself down. Her sisters' patronizing attitudes had just about gotten the best of her, but she knew in her heart that what she was doing was right. It had to be.

She wished that Gail were with her now. Gail always brought her such joy, a sense of peace, even. Even when her niece was a toddler, Peggy had been drawn to the child, and the child to her, almost to the exclusion of her own mother. But Peggy had been careful not to let her disagreements with Eva come between them, careful that they not taint their special relationship. Peggy sat at her desk and pulled out pen and paper.

Dearest Gail,

I miss you already, even though I don't get to see you enough as it is. Anytime you are away, I feel you in my heart, and I think about what you are doing, who you're making friends with, whether you are safe.

I'm sorry that I wasn't able to convince your mother to let you stay with me. I know we would have had fun, but to tell the truth, it probably would have been kind of miserable, getting bit by redbugs and scratching poison ivy. I'm sure I'll encounter plenty of both. (Although I haven't forgotten that those are also camp hazards, as well! Not to mention ghosts, although I'm sure you'll be full of scary stories to tantalize me when you get home!)

Try to make the best of your time there, honey. Camp is only an awful place if you approach it that way. Think of the friends you'll make, the good times you'll share, and the fun memories you'll have to tell your children one day.

Love always, your aunt,
Peggy

Peggy addressed the envelope and stamped it. Eva might have an out-of-sight, out-of-mind attitude toward her daughter, but Peggy was determined that her niece would always know that someone cared for her. Even if it was her mother's least favorite sister.

Otha Lee sat in a circle with the elders. This time they were meeting in Wycliffe's backyard. Lightning flashed in the distance, but it appeared the storm was heading away from them so no one seemed concerned about moving indoors.

"So, how's the church coming?" Roy sat on an old galvanized bucket, rolling a cigarette.

"Fine, just fine. Making good progress." Otha Lee sat back and hooked his finger through his suspenders. "You want to help?"

Roy shrugged. "Y'all crazy. Ain't none of us ever going to set foot in that church once all those white folks get wind of what y'all planning."

Otha Lee hesitated. A few of the group had relented some in their view of the work, at least showing a passing interest in its progress. Still, that hadn't swayed anyone over to the possibilities of the new structure, the possibility that they might have their very own holy roof over their heads come one Sunday morning.

"Give folks a chance, Roy. Sometimes people will surprise you."

"Yeah. In a white sheet, carrying a burning cross." The men nodded in agreement.

"Now we ain't had any trouble like that in years. The year 1919. Last time they lynched a Negro in this county."

"Last Negro lynched that we know about." Roy stood and exhaled a long stream of smoke. "There's Negroes missing from counties all around us, and I'll bet they been hanged right under our noses."

Otha Lee studied the young elder. "You don't know any such thing."

"Old man, you got your head buried in the sand like one of them ostriches in the desert." Roy paced around the circle. "It ain't got to be nobody 'round here doing the hanging. There's white folk out there looking to hang us niggers anywhere, anytime they got a shot at it. And you spot a herd of colored folks filing into what used to be the white man's house of worship? Might as well start digging the graves now. Not in that graveyard, either."

"Are you familiar with the expression 'putting on the full armor of God'?" Otha questioned.

"You put on that armor and they set you on fire, you just going to melt that much quicker."

"That's enough." Wycliffe walked between the two men. "Now, Brother Otha, I appreciate your dedication to this project. I believe that you believe you are doing what's right by us."

"I'm trying to do what's right by the Savior."

"So it may be. But you are putting us in danger."

"How? Has somebody threatened you all? I certainly haven't heard anything."

"No. At least not yet. Nevertheless, we all believe it would be better if we saved our money, bought our own land, and built our own church."

"How many years will that take?" Otha Lee's voice rose. "We have this opportunity, this gift, now!"

Wycliffe glanced around the circle. "Brother Otha, we have been talking. We believe you are misguided in your pursuit of this dream of yours. We respect your calling, but we no longer feel that you have been called to be our pastor."

Otha Lee rubbed his hand across his forehead. "I don't understand."

"Brother Otha, we had a meeting the other night."

"A meeting? No one let me know or I'd have been there."

"It was a meeting about you. We've decided it would be best if you stepped down as pastor."

Otha Lee laughed. "Is that what you're calling it? What you're trying to say is you're firing me." He picked his battered hat off the rocking chair and jammed it on his head.

"You're welcome to continue worshiping with us." Wycliffe stepped forward and took his hand to shake it. Otha Lee snatched it back. Roy looked down at his feet while the other men shifted in their seats, most looking at the ground.

"I thought you all were my friends. My congregation. I have sat with you through deaths, through troubles. I helped many of you during the Depression when there wasn't help to be had for colored folks. I guess it meant nothing to you."

He got into his truck and drove away, catching a glimpse of the setting sun through the pine grove that lined the road. Tears trickled from his chin, making big splotches on his white shirt.

"Dear Lord, I have prayed for hope, for guidance, for strength, and you have given it to me. Have I heard you wrong? Do you still want me as your servant?" He pulled to the side of the road and sobbed. "Maybe I am vain. Is it too much to hope for a pulpit that's out of the rain and the heat? Isn't that what you showed me through the fire? Have I traded one fire for another? Hear my prayer, Lord," he said, wiping his tears. "Show me the way, Lord. Please, show me the way."

Five

Peggy strolled into the Fourth of July celebration, knowing she would most likely run into her sisters but not really caring. Since her blowup, none of them had called or come by the house in any attempt to make up. Which suited Peggy just fine.

The upbeat atmosphere reminded Peggy of happy times with their parents when they were growing up. Her father had always designed his own fireworks display, which he set off at their cabin near the lake. Along with the sparklers from neighbors, the show often rivaled that put on by the town. Her mother, the cautious parent, always made certain they kept their distance when he lit the fuses. God forbid anyone should lose an eye or a toe or singe an eyebrow. She would never allow her children to play with sparklers, recalling the story of a childhood friend whom one had blinded, a careless accident of youth and neglectful parents.

Peggy roamed the aisles of the little fair that had sprung up overnight in the town square, which featured a statue of James Butler Bonham, the town namesake and South Carolina native famous for his role at the Alamo. Nodding to many people she knew and many she did not, she was surprised at the number of strangers who had moved into town. She made her way toward the cotton candy stand, needing a long-overdue confectionary indulgence. It surprised her to find Joseph standing there, having what appeared to be an intimate conversation with three teenaged girls. They were giggling profusely at something he had said. Peggy tried to think of anything he had said to her that was all that funny. As she ordered her candy, he turned and noticed her standing behind him.

"Oh, hey, Peggy, I didn't know you were here." He turned as if to introduce the girls and discovered they had walked away.

"I didn't mean to chase off your friends." She pulled a napkin from the dispenser to wrap around the candy stick.

"No. They were just kids. I was just funning with them."

"I thought they looked a little young."

"Why, Peggy, you make it sound as if you're getting long in the tooth, and, dear, you ain't nowhere near that." He grinned and slurped a snow cone.

Peggy stared him down, then smiled slightly. "It's just that when you get to be my age—or rather our age—anyone under the age of thirty starts looking like a toddler."

"I know what you mean." He looked down and rubbed his palm over his face. "I didn't have any business funning with those girls. I was just trying to remember what it felt like to be fresh and young and not have a past."

Peggy pondered his last comment. "A past? You? I would never have guessed." This time she grinned. Joseph had mentioned almost nothing about his life before his arrival in Bonham. In her experience, she found that usually the less a person said about their past, the more of one they seemed to have than the average person.

Joseph dug up some dirt with his toe, crumpling his snow cone cup. "Well, it's not like you were very forthcoming on that front, either."

"No, I haven't been. I guess it's because I'm your boss and you're my employee. There's an unwritten rule that dictates we stay out of one another's business."

"I wonder who dictates those rules." They sat on the gnarly roots of one of a dozen giant elms that paraded the square's perimeter. Abruptly he changed the subject. "Have you seen Otha Lee?"

"No, I haven't. He didn't show up for work again yesterday, did he?"

Joseph shook his head. Otha Lee and Joseph had begun bringing their own lunches some days, so she usually didn't bother them during their midday chats in the cemetery. Still, Otha Lee had not shown up for several days, leaving Joseph to do all the work himself, slowing the already glacial speed of the project. Peggy wondered what the problem was.

"Maybe he's just sick," said Peggy. "It has been terribly hot and he's not a young man." She waved him off. "I'm sure it's nothing. Perhaps someone in his congregation has been ill or he had some kind of church business to attend to."

"I thought maybe he had got word to you somehow." Joseph's brow wrinkled. "You reckon maybe we ought to go check on him? He could have fallen on the floor or something and nobody'd notice. I read in the newspaper the other day about some folks finding a mummified body sitting next to a radio. Man didn't have any kin or any friends. Story said he must have been there three or four years, dead, and didn't anybody know a thing about it."

Peggy shivered and reconsidered. "Maybe we should." The thought of a mummified Otha Lee reminded her of those old silent movies where mummies were always coming back to life and placing curses on people.

"Come on, Peggy," Joseph said, jumping up. "We can take my bike. It's up the street there at the rooming house."

As they walked down the street, they heard the high school band tuning up, preparing for the Independence Day parade. It brought back good memories for Peggy. She had played the flute in the band and the school orchestra. She had been quite good, winning some solo competitions. But like most youthful pursuits, Peggy had left this one behind. She was not even sure where she had stored her flute or what kind of condition it would be in by now.

Joseph straddled the bike, kicking the starter. It roared, making Peggy jump.

"You know, we can just take my car," she said, eyeing the cycle hesitantly.

"Where's the fun in that? This way we'll catch more of a breeze."

Peggy looked down at her full skirt. "I can't ride it," she shouted over the racket. "I'm wearing a dress."

Joseph took her in, noting the way the skirt set off her tanned legs. "Don't tell me you ain't never rode a motorcycle before." She shook her head. "There ain't anything to riding this thing in a dress. Just tuck it betwixt your legs."

"But once I get on, what do I hang on to?"

Joseph spread his arms and grinned. "Peggy, you just hang on to me."

She did as Joseph instructed, pulling the dress tight around her legs so the world wouldn't get any unnecessary views. Joseph glanced over his shoulder. "Ready?" he said, when he felt she was positioned. The cycle lurched away and soon left a blue trail of exhaust on the deserted road out of town.

"Peggy?" Joseph yelled over the engine noise.

"What?"

"Your fingernails are cutting into my skin."

"What?"

"Loosen your grip a little. You ain't gonna fall off."

Peggy set her chin on Joseph's shoulder and tried to relax. She never realized before what a muscular man he was. She could barely reach around his waist. She was afraid that if she didn't link her hands, she might lose her sweaty grip and go tumbling off the back into a broken-limbed, rag-doll ball.

Thankfully they soon pulled into Otha Lee's yard. The chickens flew off in a clucking flutter at the arrival of Joseph's peculiar machine. Joseph grabbed Peggy's hands and slowly released them from his shirt.

"For crying out loud, woman. No need to maul a man just 'cause he don't use a traditional form of transportation."

Peggy dusted her skirt. "I'm sorry. I guess I was more afraid than I thought."

They inspected the yard. Otha Lee had parked his truck in front of the small barn.

"Strange," Peggy said, walking up the front steps. "A day like this, Otha Lee is usually sitting on the porch fanning and swatting gnats." She knocked on the screen door. The main door was open, but seeing inside with the sun's glare coming from behind them was difficult.

"Otha Lee, you in there?" Joseph peered through a side window.

"I think we better just go on in. Something's not right." Peggy opened the screen door, which creaked loudly on unoiled hinges. Stacks of newspapers and magazines and boxes of Bible tracts lined the walls.

"Sure isn't worried about fire," said Joseph, running his hand over a disheveled pile. He looked in the kitchen and found the counter covered with dirty pots and leftover food. "Rats and flies, neither."

A door at the end of a short hall stood open. Peggy peeked in and caught her breath.

Otha Lee lay in the middle of the bed—several empty whiskey bottles, some broken, some standing, some fallen, lay scattered across the floor. He was singing quietly, his eyes raised to the ceiling. Joseph picked up some bottles and placed them on the dresser. "I never would have pegged Otha Lee for one to go on a drunk."

Peggy approached the bed. Suddenly Otha Lee sat up, realizing he was not alone.

"What y'all doing here? Sneak up on a man while he's resting." He laid back down and started whistling.

"Is that what you're calling it?" Joseph put his hand over his mouth to hide his smile. Peggy swatted him on the arm.

"Otha Lee, what's wrong? Why are you drinking? Men of God don't drink."

Otha Lee turned his head and pointed at Peggy. "Why are you yelling at me like I'm deaf? I ain't deaf," he muttered. He pushed himself up on one elbow. "Ain't you heard? I ain't no man of God no more. I done been give over to the devil."

"Go make some coffee," Peggy murmured to Joseph. "If he's got any."

"I will if I can find the pot in all that mess." He shuffled toward the kitchen, his shoulders quaking with suppressed laughter.

"Otha Lee, what is wrong with you?" Peggy perched gingerly on the bed's edge. "What are you going on about? We don't have time for this. We have a church to restore."

"I ain't working on no more church."

"It's going to be yours, remember?" She glanced around the room, trying not to breathe in the stench. "Why are you drinking? I've never known you to do this before." She began carefully picking up broken shards of glass.

"Bring me 'nother bottle, Miss Peggy. I want to forget." His voice trailed off. "Got to forget."

"Forget what? Tell me."

"I ain't got a church no more. They done walked away."

"Who walked away?"

"My elders. Say they don't want me to pastor no more. They think I'm crazy."

"Crazy?"

"For trying to take over a white man's church. Trying to give our church a home." He began to whimper.

"Now, it can't be that bad. Sit up here, Otha Lee, and let's talk about it."

"Ain't sitting up. Never. Going to stay right here in this bed 'til the Judgment Day."

"Joseph, come here!" Peggy shouted.

"What's wrong? Is he dead?" Joseph rushed in, carrying a disassembled percolator.

"Help me get him out of bed. Go around to the other side."

"Y'all ain't taking me out of my own bed. Leave me 'lone." Otha Lee closed his eyes and turned on his side.

Peggy grabbed one of Otha Lee's arms and motioned for Joseph to grab the other.

"When's the last time you went to the outhouse?" Peggy spotted a slop jar in the corner and wrinkled her nose. Joseph let go for a second to grab a handkerchief from his pocket.

"Can't remember. Last week." He wove around as Peggy tried to steady him.

"Stand up."

"Ain't gonna do it." He set his face like a recalcitrant child.

"Then we'll just do the standing for you," Joseph said. He pulled on Otha Lee to force the drunken man to his feet. "Let go of him, Peggy, I got him."

"You sure?"

"Yeah. Go ahead of me and open the door. When I get him out, go around and open some more windows. It stinks to high heaven in here."

"It sure ain't heaven here," said Otha Lee. "It's done gone to—" He cackled for a few seconds before dissolving into a hacking cough.

"You think we ought to take him to the doctor?" Peggy noted his yellowed eyes and wavering stance.

"No. Nothing a trip to the privy, a pot of coffee, some home cooking, and a good night's rest won't cure." Joseph steadied Otha Lee as they picked their way down the rickety back steps. "Way things look around here, though, I think we may have misdirected our construction efforts."

Peggy nodded. She could feel the rotten boards beneath her feet as she picked her way back to the bedroom. She quickly stripped the bed, dumping the soiled linens on the back porch before returning to rifle through the dresser drawers for some clean sheets. Noticing an old faded photograph on top of the dresser, she paused to study the fresh young face. She knew that Otha Lee's wife had died young and that he had never remarried. She returned the photograph to the dusty surface and resumed her search. In the bottom drawer she found a worn but clean set of bed linens under a bundle of letters postmarked Detroit and held together by a rotting rubber band. Next to them was a second photograph, one of a young man dressed nattily in a suit and bow tie and bearing a close resemblance to Otha Lee. Curious as to the content of the letters but worried about the ethical and moral implications of stealing Otha Lee's mail, she reluctantly put them back and began making the bed.

When she finished, Peggy retrieved the remains of the percolator and went into the kitchen, where she soon found a bag of coffee beans and an old grinder that had seen better days. She looked into the backyard and saw Joseph waiting outside the outhouse door, leaning against a chinaberry tree, whistling.

Joseph was scrutinizing Otha Lee's modest dwelling when he caught sight of Peggy looking for them through the screen door. He almost wished he had come here alone rather than put Peggy in the position of seeing her friend in such an unseemly and vulgar condition. Joseph knew that ladies shouldn't be exposed to such sights, and Peggy, he now decided, was a definite lady, one of the few he had ever encountered, the others having their noses stuck in the air as they passed him on the street.

Funny thing was, Peggy didn't seem to mind it at all. She had taken charge of the situation handily. It was strange about women, he mused. Just about the time you thought they were made of the most fragile crystal, it turned out they had the structure of a steel beam—straight and solid, able to stand heat, weight, rust, and the pounding of mallets.

The outhouse door swung open and Otha Lee staggered into the sunshine, blinking hard.

"'Bout used up my Sears catalog."

Joseph laughed. "We'll have to hunt you up a new one. I betcha Peggy's got one laying around her house somewhere."

Otha Lee suddenly lost his footing and fell to the ground before Joseph could catch him. The old man started crying.

"Miss Peggy. She's been so good to me. Offering to give me that church. And I go and disappoint her in spite of everything."

Joseph sat beside the bawling man and patted his shoulder.

"It ain't so bad. We'll keep working on it. Your elders will come around."

Otha Lee's shoulders shook as the tears made big blotches on his stained shirt. "No, they won't. They done throwed me out."

Joseph rubbed his chin. "Then you'll just start a new church."

"Say what?" Otha Lee pulled out a filthy bandanna and wiped his face.

"You say you lost your church. Well, great day in the morning, you ain't got to stick with them same old folks. World's full of sinners," he said, spreading his arms. "Take me. The Lord's going to take one look at me come Judgment Day and toss me straight in the reject pile."

"Get on! You ain't no bad man. If you was such a bad man then why are you building on a church?"

"I don't know." Joseph chewed thoughtfully on a blade of grass. "Needed the work for one thing. Or maybe that's my way of trying to get saved."

Otha Lee studied him through watery eyes. "I'd tell you to confess, but I ain't much of a preacher man right now." He looked down at himself. "Right now I'm a poor excuse for a human being."

"We'll fix that." Joseph grabbed Otha Lee's arm and helped him up, supporting him as they went back in the house. "Peggy's in there brewing some coffee and trying to scare up some supper. 'Fore you know it, you might just be a brand-new man."

"Maybe. Right now might be a good time to throw the old man out."

Peggy stood at the kitchen sink, scrubbing a pot so hard that Joseph thought he saw steam rising.

"You gonna wear the finish off that pot," he said, helping Otha Lee to a chair. He could smell the coffee percolating and the aroma of boiling grits.

"You got any bacon, Otha Lee?"

"Out in the packhouse. Y'all go on home now. You ain't got to do all this. I ain't worth the effort."

Peggy threw the dishrag in the sink, splashing suds against the window. She leaned over the table and glared at Otha Lee, who had now buried his face in his hands.

"You look at me, Otha Lee. You and I had a bargain. You help me fix up that wreck of a church and you could have it, free and clear."

Joseph walked back in with a slab of bacon and started looking for a skillet. Peggy turned around and banged one onto the stove top, causing both men to jump.

"Hell hath no fury," Joseph mumbled.

"What did you say?" Peggy now fixed her glare on Joseph.

"I said, don't worry, it's all going to work out just fine. Otha Lee's going to get himself a brand-new flock." He tested the heat and began carefully laying strips of bacon in the pan. "I told him he could preach to me."

"He needs his congregation back." Peggy stirred the grits and went back to washing dishes.

"I don't set much store by a congregation that walks out on its preacher when he ain't done nothing but try to do what's right."

"He has been preaching to those folks for a long time. There has to be some kind of spirit of forgiveness among them."

A wail rose from the table. Otha Lee was crying again.

"Oh, Otha Lee, I'm sorry." Peggy pulled up a rickety chair and put her arm around his quivering shoulders. "It'll be all right. I'll get your congregation back for you. You just worry about getting straightened out here so you and Joseph can get back to work next week."

"I ain't coming back."

Peggy grabbed him by both shoulders and shook him vehemently. Joseph placed a hand on her arm. "You don't want to do that to a man what's been on a seven-day drunk."

"I'm sorry, Miss Peggy. I know y'all just trying to help a pitiful old man," Otha Lee said between sobs.

"You are not pitiful, and you're not old," Peggy whispered. "You're just having a setback. Once you get straightened out, everything will look different."

"That's right, Otha Lee. We got a long way to go, and I ain't about to do it all by myself." Joseph winked at Peggy. "Besides, Miss Nickles here ain't got no official preaching license."

Otha Lee tried to smile and focused on the cup of strong black coffee Peggy set before him. "I reckon I am being selfish. And I did promise you, Miss Peggy." He took a cautious sip, then tipped some into his saucer and blew on it.

Peggy set three places and put the pot of grits in the table's center. Joseph poured some coffee in the frying pan to make red-eye gravy.

They sat. "Miss Peggy, you best say the grace." Otha Lee wiped his face and bowed his head.

"Dear heavenly Father, we ask you to come in and place your healing hand on our friend. He has suffered a great disappointment, and he feels discouraged, but we do not believe he is without hope. We believe we can do all things through him that strengthens us. So bless this food and this gathering, and bring Otha Lee back to us and you. In Jesus' name we pray, Amen."

"Amen!" Joseph boomed.

"Amen." Otha Lee ate slowly and wondered what he had done to deserve so much care and such kindness.

Otha Lee sat in the twilight, fanning flies and watching lightning bugs flick on and off in the falling darkness.

Peggy and Joseph had spent much of the day cleaning his house—washing clothes, scrubbing floors, burning trash. All on a Sunday, too, and the Fourth of July. As he sobered up, he felt ashamed that Miss Peggy had seen him in such a dissipated condition. He had often preached about the plague of drunkenness, but he had never revealed his own youthful history of such intemperate behavior.

He had felt lost after the elders' meeting. Not only lost from the church, but from his wife and son . . . and from God. He knew that was where he should have sought comfort and solace, and he had called out to his heavenly Father, but it seemed as if God could not be found. Otha Lee remembered the high spirits of his drunken youth and thought maybe he could find that place again.

It hadn't felt that way this time, though. The only thing he could remember of the past few days were strange visions and imaginings, seeing the elders turn their faces, closing his wife's eyes for the last time, waving good-bye to his infant son.

He stood wearily, went inside to the dresser, and opened the bottom drawer. Seeing the bundle of letters, he closed it again quickly. He slowly took off the clean clothes that Joseph had helped him into, got into the fresh bed that Peggy had made in her neat, caring way, and lay down.

"Lord and Father, please help me to forget the past and look forward to the future. You have shown me the way, and I know it is narrow. Please help me not to stray again."

He fell into the most restful sleep he had had in years.

Joseph settled into the faded upholstered chair he had purchased at the secondhand furniture store. The heat of the day and the extended effort to get Otha Lee and his house squared away had worn him down. He felt it in his bones. Working on a church wasn't nearly as tiresome as working on another human being.

The fireworks display was in full swing when he and Peggy had arrived back in the town square. They had nearly forgotten that it was still the Fourth of July. As the bright colors burst and swirled and exploded above the crowd, they had leaned against the motorcycle, quiet and reserved, neither willing to talk about the day's events.

"It is beautiful, isn't it?" Peggy tipped her head back to take in the view.

"Reminds me of a pinwheel, with the colors all mixed up in the wind."

Lightning flashed in the distance, nature adding her own fireworks to the man-made display. The crowd cheered. Soon the rumblings of thunder outbid the fireworks' blasts, and the crowd dispersed, some walking home, some riding on bicycles, still others piling into the beds of pickup trucks. Joseph walked Peggy to her car.

"Thank you for all your help today with Otha Lee," Peggy said, offering her hand. Joseph held it gently.

"I've kind of grown to like the old man. He's got a lot of thinking stored up. I think he's lonesome for somebody to share it with."

"I know." Peggy got in the car and rolled down the window. "He's important to me. I don't know just how to explain it, but I feel like he knows what's inside me without my having to say anything."

Joseph backed away from the car as Peggy gunned the engine. "Be careful. Looks like a gully-washer coming."

"I will." Peggy smiled. "See you at work."

"Yeah."

Now as the rain beat against the windows and roof, Joseph thought about Peggy and Otha Lee. With Joseph, she seemed hesitant to let her guard down, to express much other than orders or requests or obvious concerns. Yet with Otha Lee, she seemed less guarded. It was as if her feelings were stored away in a mysterious third floor room that she always kept locked. Only Otha Lee seemed to have the key.

It was like they had the same dream, too. That by rebuilding the neglected church, each might find something, something both were missing in their souls, but Joseph didn't know what it was. Maybe he would figure it out over time.

Joseph took off his clothes and stretched out on the bed. He didn't like to take baths during thunderstorms—too much risk of being struck by lightning. He thought about how different the bike felt with a second person riding. A woman riding. How different *he* felt.

Peggy was slightly built but strong. He had felt that as her legs and arms gripped him while they tore down the country roads. Once her chestnut hair had whipped around his face, and he had breathed in the fresh scent of her shampoo. He laughed a little and felt embarrassed that he had taken her on such a ride. She must be filthy. Joseph had probably ruined her dress.

The lightning continued to flicker as Joseph dozed off, inhaling Peggy's hair, feeling her arms wrapped around his chest, feeling her lips graze softly across the nape of his neck.

Monday morning, Peggy rose early and, after a quick breakfast, dug around the garden shed until she found a hoe, a rake, and a wheelbarrow. She had dressed in shorts, heeding the weatherman's prediction of one-hundred-plus degree heat.

Over the weekend, she had surveyed the progress on the church and wondered what else she could do to help. Her contribution had been little more than monetary—she had found that as a carpenter she was more a hindrance than a help. Joseph and Otha Lee were still left with the bulk of the labor. And since their distaste for her cooking had grown so obvious, she had on occasion taken to buying them hamburgers from a nearby grill instead of poisoning them herself.

Wandering the grounds, she tripped over one briar, then another. Brambles, vines, and pine and gum saplings covered the graveyard. Chinaberry branches blown out by last night's storm littered the stones. The physical work of restoring the church building itself was taking all of the men's time and would probably take the rest of the summer. Peggy knew there was no way they would ever get to the graveyard. She had decided to tackle it herself.

The cemetery dated to the early 1800s. Peggy knew that some of her ancestors were buried here, but she didn't know who they were or if their grave markers were standing or even legible by now. Perhaps the graves were unmarked. She had always been curious about these ancestors, what kind of people they were, what they had done with their lives, where they had come from. Yet the older folks she had asked showed a marked reluctance to relate any details from the past. After several aunts, uncles, and cousins refused to tell her about her kin, she had given up. Perhaps by excavating the smothered stones, she could excavate the past.

She grabbed the hoe and hacked at the edge of the ankle-twisting thicket, thankful that kudzu had not invaded this cemetery as it had so many others. She had worked for about an hour when Otha Lee's truck rolled into place. Peggy propped the hoe against a granite pillar that was taller than she was and pulled off her gloves. Otha Lee walked toward her, doffing his hat and holding it against his chest.

"Miss Peggy, I just wanted to say I'm sorry 'bout yesterday and not showing up for work last week. Leaving you and Joseph flapping in the breeze like that wasn't right. It wasn't right for a lady such as yourself to see anybody in the kind of shape I was in."

Peggy mopped her neck with a handkerchief. It was only 8:00, but the air already felt as thick as a steam bath. "There's no need to apologize, Otha Lee. You were going through a rough time." She sighed. "We all fall apart at times. Sometimes I think we need to so we can put things back together the way they're supposed to be. Here's a good example," she said, gesturing toward the church.

"Maybe you got a point." Otha Lee fanned himself with the hat. They turned at the roar of Joseph's motorcycle.

"How y'all doing?" Joseph yelled, parking the bike under a spreading oak at the cemetery's edge.

"Better'n I was the other day," Otha Lee replied. "I want to thank both of y'all for your kindness in cleaning up my house and feeding my pigs and chickens."

"That's some mighty fine swine you got there," Joseph said, grinning and hoisting a couple of two-by-fours. "Pity to see 'em go to ruin."

"It was nothing, Otha Lee," said Peggy, picking up the hoe.

"Miss Peggy, what you doing out here in this old graveyard?" Otha Lee asked.

"What does it look like?" she said, attacking a gum seedling. "I'm cleaning it up."

Joseph scratched his head. "You got one mean job there. You're gonna wear yourself out."

"I have to do something. I'm tired of sitting in the house all day watching you two have all the fun."

"Fun? Have we been having fun, Otha Lee?"

Otha Lee chuckled. "I reckon if we ain't, we better start now." He grabbed a bucket of nails and followed Joseph into the church.

Thunder pounded in the distance as the afternoon ended. Otha Lee and Joseph had knocked off early, driven away by the oppressive heat. Peggy had stopped before lunch, drenched in sweat and covered with dust.

She had made some progress, although she only managed to clear about five graves. She estimated the old cemetery must contain around two hundred or so graves; as she suspected, several were unmarked. Of the ones that were, many names were unfamiliar, although the tombstones seemed almost new. She wondered what had happened to the families, why no one had come to keep the graves cleaned or bring any memorial flowers.

Peggy's parents had been buried in the town cemetery. Actually they were entombed in a large family mausoleum her sisters insisted on having constructed. Peggy hated it. Although it was in the cemetery's most beautifully landscaped section, surrounded by dogwoods that snowed white flowers in spring and blazed with crimson foliage come fall, Peggy felt only coldness when she visited. The crypt reminded her of mummies and ancient curses. She could not bear to think of her parents in that cold marble box, NICKLES chiseled in gothic letters above the wrought-iron door.

After taking a bath, Peggy settled in front of a rattling fan in the living room. She wished the house were air conditioned, refrigerated like the movie theater. It would come in handy during this heat wave that threatened to stretch on endlessly.

A reply from Gail lay on the end table. Peggy opened the neatly addressed envelope—in spite of her spoken grammar,

Gail had learned excellent penmanship and knew how to write a proper letter. But Peggy would have been happy if it had been a "Wish you were here" scribbled on a ragged postcard.

Dear Aunt Peggy,

I have to say that as usual you were right. I'm having fun at camp in spite of myself. We roast marshmallows every night over a fire, and I'm making a purse out of beads, like the Indians used to make. The other day I fell out of a canoe and got drenched. Everyone laughed at me, but it was okay because I thought it was funny, too.

Still, I miss you so much. I'm never home as it is. I hate the thought of going back to boarding school this fall. I'd rather go to camp, if you can believe that one. I miss everyone so much while I'm away at school. Especially you, Aunt Peggy. It seems like you're the only one who really listens to me and understands me. Mother is more interested in how I'm going to turn out than how I am right now.

There I go getting maudlin, as Mother would say. (Yes, I spelled it right. You can look it up!) Please keep writing to me, Aunt Peggy. You're the only one who does.

I love you, too,
Gail

Peggy laid the letter aside and closed her eyes, silently praying for her niece's safety and comfort. When she finished, she found herself squelching her anger against Eva. Peggy found it hard to believe that her sister could not find the time or compassion to write to her own child. Then again, she knew she shouldn't be surprised at anything Eva did, or didn't, do anymore. She went to her desk and began to write.

Dearest Gail,

I just read your letter. I'm so glad that camp is turning out better than you hoped. Keep making friends and memories. I want you to tell me everything when you get home.

I know it makes you feel sad when your mother doesn't write. She's very busy, and I'm sure you'll be getting a letter from her soon. If I could do anything to keep her from sending you away again, I would, but I'm afraid I'd have about as much success as I did keeping you home from camp. Try not to be too hard on your mother. I know she loves you. I believe she loves us all. It's just harder for some people to express their love, at least in the ways we need them to.

Peggy studied her words, wondering if she had said too much, or too little. She was tired now, too tired to think any more about it. She folded her arms and laid her head down and had nearly dozed off when the jangling phone startled her.

"Hello?"

"Peggy, it's Belva."

Peggy took a deep breath. She hadn't spoken to any of her sisters since the debacle at Eva's.

"Are you there?"

"Yes, I'm here. Is something wrong?"

"No, nothing's wrong." Belva hesitated. "Well, yes, maybe it is. Honey, Bea and I feel so bad about what happened. We know Eva shouldn't have said all those things."

"No, she shouldn't. What I do with my time, my life, and my money are my business."

"We know, honey, and we talked to Eva. She is sorry."

Peggy huffed into the phone. "If she's sorry, why are you calling and not her?"

"You know how she is. She has always had trouble admitting when she's wrong."

"So she's sorry but she can't apologize because then she would be admitting she was wrong."

"Right."

The old grandfather clock in the hall struck seven, ticking off the silence that fell between them.

"Peggy, come back to brunch Wednesday. Do it for me and Bea. Eva will come around."

Peggy sighed. "I'll think about it."

"Please do. It's at Bea's. Peggy?"

"What?"

"You know we do love you. We just worry about you."

"I know. I'm fine."

"We'll see you there?"

"Maybe," Peggy said. "I said I would think about it."

She hung up the phone and read over her letter to Gail. She hated that she had to defend the child's mother to her—Peggy wasn't sure she even believed her own words. But relationships between parents and children should be encouraged, in spite of adult disagreements. She signed the letter and addressed it before pulling out the list of things yet to be done at the church. The pews were broken, and most were not worth repairing. The pulpit was so meager. Peggy felt Otha Lee deserved a grand pulpit. She had never heard him preach, but she felt in her heart that he was a true man of God and whatever he had to say must be truly inspired.

Then there were the windows. Eight stained-glass windows— actually nine if she counted the small window over the vestibule door. Peggy had spent many hours sitting in the church, envisioning those windows. She wanted them to be awe-inspiring, worthy of the Holy Spirit and to the glory of the Lord but befitting the small country chapel.

In high school, Peggy had considered becoming an artist. Her paintings and drawings had won some small awards and praise from her teachers and classmates. However, her parents never took her talent seriously. Activities such as painting qualified as hobbies, which all society ladies needed, but they were never considered a potential source of income. After the war came, Peggy had laid her brushes and pencils aside to work for charitable causes and to volunteer, the only allowable work for women of her perceived social stature.

Back in the spring, before she had finalized her plan to give the church away, she had begun experimenting on tissue paper, with colored pencils. She would draw a design, color it in, then hang it in the bright kitchen window to see how the sun's rays captured the colors and designs. She planned a different design for each window. Otha Lee was maddeningly apathetic on the matter, his thoughts having latched onto the potential topic of his first sermon, which Peggy feared would be preached to a congregation consisting solely of her and Joseph.

Taking the drafts from the buffet drawer, she spread them on the dining room table. For one window, she had depicted Paul's conversion on the road to Damascus, the bright light blinding him as the voice of the Lord raised him to the state of amazing grace. On another, Jesus calming the storm on the Sea of Galilee as the frightened disciples cowered in the rocking boat.

There was Jacob, dreaming of the angels ascending and descending the ladder. Shadrach, Meshach, and Abednego standing strong in the fiery furnace. The three kings with their gifts of gold, frankincense, and myrrh. Noah, loading the animals, two by two, on the ark made of gopher wood. For the vestibule window, Jesus' ascension into heaven, hands outstretched, beckoning the saved and the seeking.

Peggy had contacted a company in Charleston that specialized in stained glass and scheduled an appointment for Thursday. She disliked taking long trips alone and wished Roxie didn't have to work so she could go with her. That could have its drawbacks, though. Any town with sailors, and Peggy might not have an escort back.

She thought about asking Otha Lee to go—after all, they were going to be his windows. Yet a black man and a white woman traveling together would certainly draw comments and hateful looks, maybe worse. Peggy was not worried so much for herself as for Otha Lee. A white woman generally would be left alone. Nevertheless, the Negro man was always suspect, unless he was a chauffeur. What with the goings-on in Alabama and Mississippi, Peggy did not think it wise to draw unnecessary attention. That was going to come soon enough. The number of people aware of her plan to donate the church to a colored congregation was growing daily. She was not naive enough to imagine it wouldn't cause repercussions.

Joseph had proven helpful with Otha Lee. As she watched him work each day, she felt that her immediate trust in him had not been displaced. The feeling of leaning against his strong back on the motorcycle passed briefly through her thoughts, but she shooed it away. He was her friend now. A good friend.

Peggy decided she would ask him when she got the chance. It would be a simple day trip, no overnight stay, not likely to arouse anyone's suspicions and, hopefully, not gossip or speculation.

Her sisters had given up long ago on trying to fix her up. The town had few eligible men when she was younger and even fewer now. At various times she had been introduced to "appropriate" matches from Charleston, Columbia, Savannah, or Aiken—even Atlanta. It all proved wearing and superficial until she declared herself an official old maid. From time to time there were subtle suggestions from her sisters and even Roxie—especially Roxie—but she had simply given up. If she could not have a man interested in more than getting ahead financially or at least interesting enough to carry on intelligent conversation for the next forty years, she didn't want him.

Peggy Nickles had decided that being alone was better than being lonely with someone else.

Wednesday morning, in Beatrice's living room, Peggy sat making small talk about the pounding heat with her sisters. The heat wave had grown into a stretch of ninety and one hundred degree-plus days, provoking the movie theaters into offering extra showings even on weekdays when folks would ordinarily be working. Joseph had admitted to a few afternoon matinees, as had Otha Lee, who ordinarily didn't attend movies on account of all the shenanigans that went on among teenagers in the colored balcony. However, he soon found his presence was a deterrent to such behavior and so had increased his attendance.

Peggy fanned herself. Beatrice's house was in an advanced state of renovation, including the installation of a very expensive central air-conditioning system. It was to be the first house in Bonham to sport such an amenity and was the topic of hot conversation around town and among the sisters. Peggy had toyed with the idea of having it installed in the church, but Otha Lee balked, arguing that people should not be too comfortable in church, lest they forget the hellfire that awaited if they did not heed the words of God.

Peggy and Eva sat opposite each other on the thinly cushioned Danish Modern furniture, sweating and looking at everything but each other. Peggy wished she hadn't come, but Belva had called again and insisted. She had to admit that the twins hadn't bothered her as much as Eva, and she did miss seeing them. She felt she could tolerate Eva for their sakes; still, she didn't know how they would ever heal their rift, or even if she wanted to. Peggy and Eva were separated not only by age but by temperament, although Peggy realized they possessed the same stubborn streak, which probably made them more alike than different.

"How is that handyman working out?" Beatrice asked quietly after Eva and Belva left the room for another tour of the house to discuss wallpaper and drapery fabrics.

"He's doing just fine. He does good work, and he gets along well with Otha Lee."

"Good." Beatrice sipped her tea. The ice tinkled in the crystal goblet and the lemon wedge bobbed in its icy pool. "How *is* Otha Lee?"

"The heat's getting to him. They're only working half days. Joseph stays around some days to help me with the cemetery."

"What are you doing at the cemetery?" Beatrice placed her tea on the coffee table and turned to face Peggy with interest.

"Cleaning it up. It's nothing more than a weed patch right now. You can't even tell it's a cemetery in spots."

"Well, why don't you just leave that alone? No one's going to be using it anymore." Beatrice giggled at her own wisecrack.

Peggy frowned. "Because it will improve the looks of the place. Besides, our ancestors are buried there. Wouldn't you like to know more about them?" She adjusted the oscillating fan so it would blow on them directly. "I certainly would."

"You're not planning to let the colored bury their dead there now, are you?"

Peggy didn't answer.

"Are you?" Bea's voice rose, attracting Eva and Belva's attention.

"Are you what?" Belva asked, readjusting the fan.

Peggy smiled at her sisters. "Let Otha Lee conduct funerals in the church cemetery."

Beatrice gasped. Belva sat heavily, throwing the chair off balance before she caught it.

"I knew it," Eva said. "She's about to cause a race riot."

"There are already Negroes buried there. The church records say there's a slave section somewhere in all that brush."

"That was then and this is now, Peggy," Belva said.

"Since when did the descendants care? They—or I should say, we, seeing how we are the descendants of the church—let the graves grow up in weeds. No one's laid flowers there in years. They sold the church, for goodness' sake! To me. When did you ever hear of that happening?"

"Calm down, dear," Belva said, placing her hand on Peggy's shoulder.

"The descendants of the church will never allow it," Eva said.

"In case you weren't listening," Peggy said quietly and steadily, "we *are* the descendants of the church."

"I know," Eva said. "I heard you."

"So what are you planning to do?" Peggy asked, with fire in her eyes.

"I'm not sure yet. I have a lawyer looking into it." Eva sat down in a spare rocker and began rocking back and forth. Peggy leveled a look at Belva.

"Is this what you got me here for?"

Before Belva could answer, Eva broke in. "It's for your own good, Peggy. Daddy and Mother wouldn't want you wasting your resources like this."

"What? Spending my money to the glory of God?"

"Glory of yourself is more like it." Eva stopped rocking and leaned forward. "This is not about God and you know it. It's about guilt."

Peggy picked up her bag and went to the door. "You don't know anything about it, Eva."

Eva followed her out to the car. "You think about it, little sister. You know I'm right."

Peggy glared at her. "And that's always the way, isn't it. You know everything, and we know nothing. But I know this." She walked back around the car and pointed a trembling finger in Eva's face. "The church is mine now, and it is going to be Otha Lee's when it's finished. So is the cemetery. You can call all the lawyers and judges in this town, but you're not stopping us." She took a deep breath. "I guess what the Bible says is true."

"You're going to quote Scripture at me now?" Eva watched her with a bemused expression.

"A man's enemies are the men of his own house." Peggy turned to go, tears streaming down her face. "I guess that goes for women, too."

seven

Joseph leaned against the spreading oak tree in Peggy's front yard, chewing a blade of grass. Peggy had asked him to accompany her to Charleston, and he felt a little nervous. For one thing, he had never been to Charleston, or anywhere for that matter, with a woman driving. He had never been anywhere with a woman like Peggy, period. But that was just a small part of his unease.

He had consulted a map at the gas station the night before and discovered they would be driving within five miles of where he thought he could never go again. It had been so many years since he had been there. Once it was a place familiar and loved. Now it was a place he dreaded and feared, a place he had vowed never to lay eyes on again.

The place was home.

Joseph hadn't been back there in twenty years. He knew Mama was still alive. A few acquaintances in Columbia had passed through the small community where she lived, stopping at the small truck stop she ran. His daddy had died ten years ago; his mother had let him know that at least. A sudden heart attack on a hot day in the middle of a cornfield.

As to his sister's whereabouts, Joseph had no idea. She had left home before he did, and he didn't know if she had kept in touch with Mama. He wished he could see her again. They had been close as children, but she had changed as a teenager, becoming a stranger to everyone, most especially him.

Brett. His brother. Joseph knew where he was.

Buried in an old country cemetery, much like the one next to the church. Probably grown over now with trees and briars, the headstone chipped and worn away by weather and time. He longed to visit the grave but knew he couldn't ask Peggy to take him. It would demand too many revelations. Driving through the county would be conspicuous enough in that long blue Caddy. He didn't want to risk any needless encounters.

"Ready to go?" Peggy bounded down the steps wearing a blue cotton dress and a wide-brimmed straw hat. She was carrying a long cardboard tube.

"What's in there?"

"Designs for the windows. You'll see them when we get there." She tossed the tube in the backseat and threw the keys to Joseph.

"You want me to drive?"

"You do know how to drive a four-wheeled vehicle, don't you? You did manage to get me to Otha Lee's and back alive." She smiled slyly.

"Yeah, I've driven plenty of four-wheeled vehicles, but I never piloted a boat before." He surveyed the car's length and breadth, running his hand across the rounded tailfin.

Peggy studied her newly appointed chauffeur. She had never seen him in anything other than dungarees and T-shirts. She had to admit he cleaned up nicely in his pressed chinos, starched white shirt, and buffed loafers. His darkening tan accentuated those steel-gray eyes.

Joseph realized she was staring at him. He felt his chin to see if he remembered to remove the toilet paper he had used to mop a shaving nick.

"Joseph? Let's go." Peggy sat in the passenger seat smoothing her full skirt.

He hit the starter and backed cautiously out of the driveway.

"What are you waiting for? Don't be afraid of it! Hit the gas!" Peggy was unusually animated.

"Whatever you say, Miss Peggy," Joseph replied, as the dust puffed up behind the car. "You're the boss."

Otha Lee sat on the front porch, mopping his forehead. He was almost glad they weren't working on the church today. The string of hot, humid days was taking its toll on his aging body. Joseph seemed to handle it, but then, he was younger. His body had yet to break down under such strains.

The mail had come earlier, and Otha Lee laid the stack of letters on a small table next to the rocking chair. The electricity bill, a notice of a revival at a neighboring church.

A letter. Postmarked Detroit.

He stared at the envelope, his eyes locked on the handwriting, trying to remember if it was that of his sister-in-law. It had been years since he had heard any news, and he always feared that any news he did hear would be bad. That seemed to be the bulk of the news he got.

Tapping the envelope on the chair first, Otha Lee ripped off the short end. A single page letter, typed neatly, dated two weeks earlier.

Dear Dad,

Or I guess that's what I should call you. It turns out the man I have called Daddy my whole life is not, and you are.

I only recently found out who you are, that you even exist. Mama told me about my own mother's death and why you gave me to her to raise. I just want you to know I understand, and I do not have any bad feelings toward you.

The reason I am writing is that I would like to meet you. I have been teaching at the local university (I am a history professor), but I am taking the fall semester off to research a book. Part of that research involves looking into my past. I guess that's why Mama told me about you, because you are a part of that past.

I hope to be coming down there sometime in August. I would have called you, but Mama said she didn't think you had a telephone. I will write to you again soon and let you know my travel plans.

I am looking forward to getting to know you, Dad.

> *Yours very truly,*
> *Otis Jackson*

"Praise God in heaven, he's alive," Otha Lee said, closing his eyes. "He's alive and wants to know me. Thank you, Jesus."

It was the happiest news he had heard in years, greater even than Miss Peggy's offer of the church. He ran down the steps and danced among the scattering chickens. "Otis is coming home!" he shouted to the hogs, who blinked and continued their peaceful relaxation in a deep mud puddle.

He stopped under the chinaberry tree and caught his breath. Sweat rolled down his nose. Wiping it off, he read the letter again. Placing it back in the envelope, he took it inside and propped it against the photograph of his beloved Esther. "Our boy's coming home," he said, his fingers grazing the faded image.

Falling to his knees, he folded his hands in front of his heart. "Dear Lord," he said as tears replaced sweat, "thank you for this gift. Watch over my boy as you have all these years. Help me not to be a disappointment to him. Let me make it up to him—the time, the years. Oh, heavenly Father, your mercies are great. Amen."

Otha Lee rose carefully and fingered the letter again. He set it aside and walked into the living room, looking at his home with new clarity of vision. What a mess of papers he had accumulated. When Peggy and Joseph cleaned up, they had concentrated mainly on the bedroom and the kitchen. Now Otha Lee realized how much remained to be done. He didn't want his college professor son thinking his father lived like trash. This wasn't fitting for a garbage man, much less a man of the cloth.

And what would his son think, returning home to find a preaching father who was a shepherd without a flock? He fell to his knees again.

"Heavenly Father, I got to ask for something else. I need my congregation back. Help me find a way to get them back. If not for me, Lord, for Otis."

Pacing back and forth, through and around the house, Otha Lee made mental notes of everything that needed doing. He had a little money saved from selling his hogs last winter, but he didn't know how far that would go toward patching the leaky tin roof or shoring up the rickety porch. It had been years since the house had a new coat of paint, inside and out. Suddenly, he felt dizzy and turned on the box fan, which sent a pile of Bible tracts scooting across the room like leaves before an autumn wind.

It started as a chuckle, then became a full-blown belly laugh. Otha Lee laughed until the tears streamed, then cried until he laughed again.

He couldn't wait for Miss Peggy and Joseph to get back. Right now what this place needed was a woman's touch . . . and a young man's back.

Joseph drove slowly through the narrow streets of Charleston, feeling as if he had stepped back a hundred years. Passing through the low country, they had felt the humidity rise with each mile. By the time they reached their destination, Joseph felt as if he were breathing underwater, swimming deeper and deeper, the pressure crushing his lungs and the dampness saturating his clothes.

Beside him, Peggy wore a perplexed look. Her earlier animation seemed to wither under the sultry air. Although Charleston was familiar to her, the site of many youthful happy times, its historical atmosphere reminded her of nearly forgotten sorrows. The gray Spanish moss dripped from the trees like witches' hair, the texture of steel wool, waving in the scanty sea breezes.

At Peggy's direction Joseph pulled into a short side street, where a small shop was sequestered, accessible through an intricate wrought-iron gate festooned with depictions of marsh birds and sea grasses. A bookstore hawking used rare editions and a basket seller stacked to the rafters with sea-grass baskets flanked the shop.

Joseph grabbed the tube from the backseat and followed Peggy up the tabby-paved walk. She rang a bell hanging next to the carved door, and a short, curly-haired man wearing a black apron over his clothes and thick work gloves greeted them warmly. He introduced himself as Hampton St. Berthier, Hamp for short.

Peggy gasped as she entered the workshop. Leaning against the walls and laying on the tables were collections of stained-glass windows, many far more intricate and colorful than anything she had dreamed of in her church-bound musings. All manner of birds, mammals, reptiles were depicted in colors that no rainbow could duplicate. She walked about, reaching toward the panes of glass, but not touching should she accidentally leave a smudge to mar their polished beauty. Grabbing the tube from Joseph, she pulled out the designs and began ripping them to shreds.

"Peggy, what in the world are you doing?" Joseph tried to pull some of the sheets away from her.

"They're not good enough. They will never be good enough. I will never be good enough." Pieces of paper flew from her hands like confetti. Hamp stood to one side, his arms folded, as if he had seen this type of behavior before.

Joseph grasped her arms, trying to still her fury. "Peggy, what's gotten into you?" he asked quietly. "You were so excited this morning. What's wrong with your windows?"

Peggy crumpled the drawing she held into a tight ball and threw it across the room. She broke free of his grasp and spread her arms. "Look around. I'm no artist."

Hamp gathered the crumpled drawings while Peggy sank into a chair, covering her eyes.

"I beg to differ," he said, smoothing out the paper, tracing lines with a pudgy finger. "These are magnificent."

"They're childish. A kindergarten child could come up with something more original," she said, pouting.

"You have to remember that this is just paper and pastels. Not glass." Hamp held one up to the light. "What you have drawn will translate wonderfully into the stained-glass medium."

Joseph picked up the shreds and began piecing them back together. Hamp handed him a roll of cellophane tape.

Peggy continued to sit in the chair and sulk. "Otha Lee deserves more than that. He deserves the work of a true artisan. Not scribblings from an amateur."

"Are you familiar with the Cathedral of Chartres, in France? The windows?" Hamp held another drawing at arm's length.

"No," Peggy said, sniffling.

Hamp went to a drawer and pulled out a heavy coffee-table book. Thumbing through it, he found the picture he wanted and handed it to Joseph. "Would you say hers compare?"

"Yeah, I'd say they would," Joseph replied, letting out a low whistle. "The little old town of Bonham don't know they've got a genuine artist living there."

"Miss Nickles, you deeply underestimate yourself. The intricacy of these designs is stunning. It will be a challenge to translate them into the finished windows." A slow smile spread over Hamp's face. "This man you mention—Otha Lee? He will have the work of an artist. This is work obviously done out of great joy. And great love."

Joseph knelt in front of Peggy and took her hand, smoothing her hair away from her face. "You hear that, Peggy? You're an artist." Placing his hand under her chin, he tipped up her face. "Cut yourself some slack."

Peggy pulled a handkerchief from her purse and dabbed at her eyes. She looked at the shopkeeper. "I'm sorry to have become so hysterical. I guess I wasn't prepared for all this beauty. Mine seems inept in comparison."

"The only thing you should be apologetic about is that you are not doing this for a living."

Peggy came over to the table where they reassembled the drawings. "Do you really believe I have enough talent to do that? I mean, I thought you had to go to art school to become a professional."

"Most professionals have never seen the inside of an art school." Hamp laughed softly. "All you need are talent and passion, and you certainly have plenty of both."

Joseph grinned at Peggy, who managed a thin smile. Looking around, she still felt her work was inferior, but she realized the stained-glass artisan may have a point. After all, her sketches were only ideas to which he would bring his own hand. Perhaps she was being too hard on herself.

"Would you like for me to write you an estimate?" Hamp asked.

She took a deep breath. "Yes, I would."

"Perhaps you and Mr. Davidson would like to go get some lunch. There is a luncheon counter around the corner. I will have an estimate for you when you return."

"Thank you, sir; we'll do that." Joseph placed his hand lightly on Peggy's elbow and guided her out the door.

Away from the shop's industrial fans, the humidity settled back on them like wet sheets. They walked down the street, Joseph quiet, Peggy still sniffling into her handkerchief.

"You must think I'm one of those crazy hysterical females like you see in the movies."

Joseph dug his hands into his pockets. "No. I've found real-life hysterical females to be a lot more interesting."

Peggy stared at him a moment before they both broke into nervous laughter.

"The truth is, Joseph, I don't know if we're going to have a church to put these stained-glass windows in." They sat on a shaded park bench. "I haven't said much about my sisters, have I?"

"To hear Otha Lee talk, they're all a real piece of work. Said they remind him more of your mama than your daddy. He said you remind him of your daddy, though. He said it nice, like it was a compliment."

Peggy smiled. "So I'll take it as one. As for my sisters, we don't exactly agree on many things. Like the church. They objected to my buying the church to begin with. They said buying property that rightfully belonged to the Lord was unseemly for a woman, particularly a single woman."

"Yeah, but ain't somebody here on earth got to run it? I know it's the Lord's house and all, but it ain't nothing but a pile of well-placed lumber if it hasn't got a congregation."

"My thoughts exactly. It was going to ruin, and when it came up for sale as abandoned property, I was drawn to it. It was like I was being guided by a feeling I couldn't control."

"So what's your sisters' problem? It ain't like you gonna set up and go to preaching." He grinned slyly. "Or are you?" He rubbed his chin. "You ask me, women do enough preaching out in the open. They don't need a pulpit to stand behind."

Peggy swatted him on the shoulder with her purse, allowing herself a smile. "If I had known how bad you were, I might not have started this story."

Joseph rubbed his shoulder. "Lady, you pack a wallop. Now, I was just messing with you and you know it, so go on, it's past time for lunch."

"It boils down to Otha Lee. They don't think a colored congregation ought to be taking what has historically been a white people's church."

They sat silently, watching a lone sailboat drifting through the harbor.

"So what are they planning to do?"

"Take me to court."

"They can't do that. Not if you own it free and clear." Joseph's shoulder rubbed lightly against Peggy's.

"They're going on some descendants of members claim. You see, our family used to belong to the church way back when. In fact, I've been told that many of our ancestors are buried there. That's one reason I'm working on the cemetery."

"They don't really have a case, do they?"

"Joseph, I don't know. I'm going to see my lawyer Monday." She rubbed her eyes. "I've bored you long enough. Let's go get some seafood."

"I can wrap my mouth around that." Joseph turned to Peggy, placing his hands lightly on her shoulders. "Peggy, I admire what you're doing. Ain't many people these days would show the kindness you've shown to Otha Lee. Or to me."

"It's nothing, Joseph."

"Believe me, Peggy. It's a lot."

Driving home, the rain beating so hard he could barely see to drive, Joseph noticed that Peggy had lapsed back into a thoughtful silence. At Hamp's workshop, she had agreed to the price and scheduled an October delivery date. They then spent several hours driving through the low country, looking at old plantations and historic sites, Peggy providing a running monologue on South Carolina history and genealogy to rival the begats in the Old Testament.

Joseph was actually thankful for Peggy's silence, in that it masked his own. They were passing through his home county. Joseph carefully stuck to the speed limit so he wouldn't attract attention. He decided there was no need for Peggy to find out about his past just yet. She had placed her trust in him from the moment they had met, something he had experienced from few others in his life. Otha Lee was just about the same way.

"Joseph, do you believe in God?"

Peggy's sudden question threw him off balance, and he momentarily lost focus on the rain-drenched highway, hitting a large puddle that fanned water over a tired roadside mailbox.

"Where'd that come from?"

"Do you?"

"I guess I do. Can't say me and the Savior's been on speaking terms in a while, though. You ain't fixing to preach at me, are you?"

Peggy leaned her arm on the window ledge and stared at the pouring rain. "No. I was just wondering."

"Wondering what?"

"Why sometimes God seems to be so close to us and other times it feels like he's not even there at all." She pointed a finger at his chest. "And don't you go and start calling me blasphemous, either."

"I wouldn't dream of it. It's odd, though. I always thought you were stone cold solid in the faith, what with buying the church and all."

"Don't get me wrong; I believe, but sometimes I feel like I don't believe enough. Like when things start going wrong."

Joseph slowed as the rain began to blow across the hood. "I think we better pull over and wait this out." He turned into a long driveway that led up to a tobacco barn, barely visible through the deluge. He turned off the engine and looked over at Peggy.

"Shouldn't you be having this discussion with Otha Lee?"

"What, and risk getting preached at?" Peggy smiled and braced her palms on the dash. "I wish sometimes I could be more—I don't know—sure."

"Sure of what?"

"God. Heaven. Life after death."

"I thought if you were saved you got all those things wrapped up like a Christmas present." He grinned. "No pun intended, of course."

"It's not that simple, though. How can God overlook what you've done in the past? How does he overlook the wrongs of your life?"

"I don't think you got any problem on that score, Peggy. You're about the rightest woman I ever knew. Me, on the other hand. I'm the one that ought to be worried."

"Maybe we both ought to be having this conversation with Otha Lee." She peered through the windshield at the receding clouds. "Looks like it's blowing over. Let's get on home. I'm tired."

Joseph placed his hand carefully over Peggy's, feeling his palm against her smooth, cool skin. "Whatever it is you think you did wrong, believe you me, there is always somebody that's done worse. Believe me."

Peggy withdrew her hand. "Let's go, Joseph."

He pulled into the rain, now reduced to a shower, and rolled down the window, letting the cool breeze and clean smell waft over them and lull Peggy into a sound and restful sleep.

eight

"Your *who* is coming home?" Joseph gaped, hammer in hand, as Otha Lee strutted around the emerging tombstones. Peggy stood speechless.

"My son," he proclaimed proudly.

"You never mentioned a son," Joseph said.

"He's about the same age as you, Miss Peggy. Born about the same time." Otha Lee then extracted the letter from his pocket and read it as if it were the text of his next sermon.

"That must have been the picture of him I saw in the drawer," Peggy said quietly.

"What?" Otha Lee stopped in front of her.

"Oh, at your house, the day you were sick. The picture in the drawer with the sheets. The boy wearing a bow tie."

"That it was. And you meant drunk, not sick," he added, winking at Joseph.

"So when is he supposed to get here?" Joseph asked.

"August. I was wondering if you'd help me get my house fixed up, Joseph. I can't pay you what Miss Peggy's paying, but I can cook you a decent supper." He winced. "No offense, Miss Peggy."

"None taken, Otha Lee." She turned toward the house. "I have a meeting to get to. I'll probably see you this afternoon."

Joseph came to Peggy and lightly touched her arm, while Otha Lee went inside the church and began hammering. "Good luck today, Peggy."

"I think it's going to take more than luck."

"Then I'll make an exception," he said, reaching up and smoothing a stray strand of hair from her forehead. "I'll pray for you."

Peggy sat in the waiting room of Percy, Miles, and Cameron. The offices were dark and cool; the secretary noisily typed carbons on an old Remington typewriter. Peggy had been here only a few times. The reading of her parents' wills. Closing the deed on the church. The office reminded her of a funeral home, a place where people whispered quiet condolences, holding reverent the particulars and peculiarities of the law.

Milo Percy emerged from his office and motioned for Peggy to enter. Milo Percy had been a good friend of Peggy's father and Peggy trusted him deeply. With his silver hair and tall, slender stature, he reminded Peggy that chivalry lived on in Southern gentlemen who still believed in the values of respect, dignity, and honor.

Peggy sat down on a leather sofa, while Milo took a matching chair opposite. A soft breeze rustled the dark drapes.

"Let's visit, Peggy. I've cleared my calendar until lunch. Tell me how it's going with the church."

"The renovations are going quite well, but this terrible heat has slowed the pace a bit."

"I understand Otha Lee is working with you. Of course, that *was* your plan."

"Yes, and that's what I have come to talk with you about."

"Is there a problem?"

"Problems, plural."

"And their names are Eva, Belva, and Beatrice." Milo nodded thoughtfully. "Not the quarter I expected trouble from but suspected might arise."

"Oh? You were expecting trouble from someone else?"

"Men in white hoods, bearing flaming crucifixes."

"Surprise."

"It's always from the quarters one least expects, isn't it? Trouble, that is."

"Most assuredly." Peggy sighed. "They've threatened me with a lawsuit. They don't believe I own the church property legally."

Milo shifted, crossing his legs. "They believe you had poor representation in the real estate transaction?"

"No. They think I shouldn't have bought the church in the first place. They seem to believe that they should own the church. They're scared to death colored people are going to be buried there when Otha Lee takes over."

"Don't they realize the bodies of slaves lay there in perpetual rest?"

"Yes, but they were slaves. To them, it's like saying a few stray dogs or cats were buried there by mistake. They don't count somehow."

"You know, of course, that your own family owned some of those slaves." He paused, studying Peggy's eyes. "You look a little stunned. I thought you knew."

"I suppose I knew, but I hadn't really wanted to admit that my forebears actually owned other human beings."

"How much do you really know about your own family, Peggy? I don't mean now—I'm sure you feel you know far too much. I mean the past. Who they were, what they did. Their relationships. Their secrets."

"Secrets? Now you've piqued my interest." Peggy smiled. "I'm trying to figure out the past. I have been cleaning out the cemetery in drips and drabs, but the heat and bugs are making it a difficult task." She gazed into the attorney's eyes. "Why? Do you know something I should?"

Milo leaned forward and patted her hand. "We best discover some things on our own, Peggy dear. My knowledge of your family is limited to hearsay and gossip."

Peggy's eyes widened. "Were we that scandalous?"

Milo laughed. "Not scandalous. Merely behaving in accordance with the times."

"I guess I should be careful where I dig then. I wouldn't want to unleash any ghosts."

"The ghosts of the past surround us, my dear. It's learning to see them—that's the thing." He went to the chair behind his desk. "As far as your sisters go, I will review the deed and the transaction, but frankly they don't have a legal leg to stand on. I don't know of any law saying whites and coloreds can't be buried in the same sanctified ground."

"That's what I was hoping you would say."

Milo consulted his watch. "Is there anything else? I'm afraid I have to go. My Optimist Club meets at 12:30 at the country club."

"No, Mr. Percy, don't let me keep you."

"Peggy," he said, as she turned to leave. "Don't be surprised at what you discover. The past is what makes us who we are. Redemption isn't always found within the house of the Lord. Sometimes it's found in the fields of humanity."

"You mean this is going to be your church and Peggy didn't give you any say-so over the windows? Now ain't that a woman!" Joseph drank deeply from a Mason jar of water he had filled at the spigot behind Peggy's porch.

"Oh, she asked me, but it didn't make no mind to me."

"Well you are in for a treat, my friend, because Peggy yonder has turned out to be one heck of an artist." Joseph started to say hell, but realized where he was in time. He was trying to stop using swear words, particularly around Peggy and Otha Lee. He was getting his monetary act together and had no wish to offend.

"I ain't going to be looking at windows, Joseph," Otha Lee said, his eyes twinkling. "I'm going to be looking at souls to be saved. Praise Jesus!"

Joseph noticed Otha Lee was working with a new jolt of enthusiasm since learning his son would be coming home. With the heat wave dragging on, Joseph and Otha Lee went home every day with their clothing drenched. Joseph admired Otha Lee for his inner power and strength after he had come so close to losing his resolve.

He looked at Peggy, who was attacking trumpet vines with determination. Joseph kept expecting her to fall out in the endless hot days, but she too seemed driven, as if her very soul was at stake. Joseph began to feel himself infected with an unforeseen and inexplicable drive, as if his purpose in life boiled down to helping two people find a way not just to save souls but save themselves, although Joseph wasn't sure from what.

He thought back on the trip to Charleston and Peggy's unusual forthrightness in expressing her feelings. She was often so reserved that Joseph felt awkward even speaking in her presence, as if he were breaking a deep contemplative silence she seemed to use almost as a shield. For once, he hadn't felt at arm's length. In fact, he felt almost like her friend. Peggy's abrupt scream shook him out of his musings.

"Snake!" She sat on top of a tombstone, feet up, pointing to a six-foot copperhead that lay cooling in the shade.

Joseph started laughing. "Did he bite you?"

Peggy glared at him. "No, but I might just do something worse to you if you don't kill it."

Moving warily, he grasped the hoe and approached the snake, which was curling slowly into its attack coil. Joseph brought up the hoe, then struck swiftly, neatly decapitating the hissing reptile. He picked up the carcass and appraised it appreciatively.

"Know anything about cooking snakes? Maybe rousting up a little stew?"

"Very funny," Peggy said, easing off the tombstone and staring at the snake's head, half expecting it to come back to life.

Joseph flung the snake into the woods. He was certain it would provide another varmint an appetizing feast.

"Anything else you want me to kill while I'm over here?" He looked around then mockingly slapped a hand to his forehead. "I forgot. Everything's already dead."

"And you're going to be next if you don't get back to work." She pulled out a handkerchief and wiped her face. "By the way—thank you."

Joseph tipped his straw hat and bowed. "Miss Peggy, ma'am, you are quite welcome."

As he walked away, Peggy had to smile and suppressed a laugh at her own helplessness. It had been another stifling day, and she still hadn't uncovered anything significant, except the stone of her namesake, Aunt Margaret, nicknamed Peggy like herself, but who bore more of a personality resemblance to Eva.

She went to the back porch and sat at the picnic table, the box fan blowing full in her face. The church was beginning to take shape. The roof was solid now, and the floor replacement was nearly complete. Soon Otha Lee and Joseph would begin repairing the old pews and pulpit. Peggy had offered to buy new ones, but Otha Lee said his congregation was probably going to be so amazed at those fancy stained-glass windows, they wouldn't care what they were sitting on.

And Joseph. She frequently thought of their conversation in the storm, wondering why she had allowed herself to be so open with him—as open as she could be, anyway. It had been years since she had allowed herself to be truly close to anyone, and she often feared her intensifying emotions in recent weeks. She feared a return to the dark time, the time she barely recalled. That had resulted from closeness, from allowing herself to feel. Love, hate, warmth, compassion—it had taken a long time to find the will to be civil again, much less anything more.

She pondered the reason for Joseph's abrupt appearance, the day she turned and faced those deep gray eyes looking into hers across that field of weathered gray stones. Was he, too, here to help her unearth the past? Or had he simply arrived to play some unwritten role in the future? Her thoughts echoed until she felt her head was ringing, only to realize it was the phone that she was hearing.

She ran in and caught it up in her sweaty hand. "Don't hang up!"

"Aunt Peggy, I was beginning to worry."

"Gail." Peggy sat at the kitchen table, stretching the black cord across the room. "I thought you'd be off to the movies with your friends on a day like this."

Gail sighed heavily. "My friends have decided they don't want to be my friends anymore."

"What do you mean?"

"I mean just that. They're not my friends anymore!"

Peggy could hear the strain in Gail's voice. "Did something happen? Did you have a fight?"

"No," Gail said, almost whispering. "They said I'm too much of a little girl." Sniffling sounds came through the receiver. "They said if I didn't start wearing lipstick and smoking cigarettes they wouldn't be my friends."

Peggy smiled to herself, although deep inside she felt her niece's hurt. "Sweetheart, if it takes lipstick and cigarettes to keep a friend, the friend's not worth keeping. Besides, lipstick is overrated and cigarettes will kill you."

"Thanks a lot." Gail huffed into the phone. "In the meantime, what am I supposed to do? I've got the rest of the summer, Mother won't let me come stay with you, and I ain't got nobody to do anything with."

"Don't have anybody," Peggy corrected, then realized she sounded just like Eva. Self-consciousness would eventually correct Gail's grammar; she could do without the Nickles family nitpickiness. "Isn't it about time for your beach trip?"

"Oh, yes, the thrill of Mother constantly telling me, 'Put on your hat; ladies do not get suntans; this sun will ruin your porcelain skin.' I mean, Aunt Peggy, isn't that the whole point of going to the beach, to get sunburned and to get sand in your clothes?"

Peggy had to laugh at her niece's perfect mimicry of Eva, although she knew she shouldn't condone it. "It won't be so bad," Peggy said, holding back her laughter. "And think of it this way—maybe you'll meet some new friends. Don't you have a pen pal you met there last year?"

"Yeah. I guess." Gail heaved another sigh through the lines. "It's not the same, though."

"It will be okay, Gail. Friends come and go, and you'll meet a whole passel of new ones next year at school."

"A whole passel? Boy, Aunt Peggy, maybe Mother's right."

"Right about what?"

"That handyman is corrupting your manner of speaking."

Peggy ignored the jab and murmured a promise to see her niece soon before hanging up. She went outside and picked a couple of red ripe tomatoes to chill in the refrigerator while she took her bath. Since her "manner of speaking" was being compromised, she decided she might as well go all the way. A tomato sandwich eaten over the sink with the juice dripping off her elbows would be a nice end to the day. On second thought, maybe she'd better eat it before she took her bath.

nine

Otha Lee stared at himself in the mirror, wiping the last bit of shaving lather from his chin. He wanted to look immaculate. Starched white shirt, black pants, and red suspenders—he dispensed with the bow tie in deference to the heat. Jamming a new straw fedora on his head, he started for the front door.

Otis was coming home.

The house, for once in its existence, looked proud, like it was expecting company, too. He owed most of it to Peggy and Joseph's youthful energies. They had spent many hours helping him repair the porch and the roof and replace worn linens and rugs. Peggy had sewn new curtains and painted a picture of a sailing boat for him to hang over the mantelpiece. Otha Lee had to admit that a woman's touch made quite a difference.

He double-checked the second bedroom, noting the sunshine-clean smell emanating from the freshly washed sheets. A brand-new oscillating fan stood on the bedside table. Otha Lee knew it wouldn't go far toward fighting the stifling humidity, but at least it would circulate the air.

Walking around the room, Otha Lee stopped at the desk, a huge roll-topped monolith Peggy had brought out of storage and given to him for Otis. Since Otis planned to conduct research, the three agreed he should have a proper place at which to work and store his papers. An old lamp with a tattered fringe stood on top, a brand-new lightbulb waiting to illuminate the desk's polished surface.

Outside, Otha Lee inspected his humble home. The rocking chairs sported a glossy coat of green paint, and all the house trim had been painted white. He reckoned they had all spent more time on the house than the church lately, and he felt a pang of guilt for neglecting the spiritual side of events.

Removing his hat, he bowed his head. "Dear Lord," he prayed, as the chickens pecked around his feet, "I know this ain't going to be easy. My son don't know me from Adam. But we're of the same blood, and I hope that counts for something. I know you've forgiven me for letting him go. I didn't have much of a choice. So I hope you'll help him to forgive me, too. He says he don't have any hard feelings, but that's a hard thing to believe from somebody whose father's abandoned him, so to speak. So I'm hoping you'll make everything work out all right. For both of us. In Jesus' name, Amen."

He put on his hat again and got into the pickup truck. It gleamed from Joseph's washing and waxing. Otha Lee thought it looked brand new, although it had been quite used when he purchased it before the war with his hog money.

Driving into town, toward the bus station, Otha Lee waved to several members of his congregation, some of whom waved back or dissolved into whispers behind calloused hands. He had heard they were looking for a new pastor, but none had met with approval. Too much theology and not enough spirit, one of the regulars at the barbershop had told him.

Parking at the station, Otha Lee saw the bus approach. He went to the "Colored" platform and waited. The bus squealed to a stop, emitting a loud hiss as the doors popped open, as if releasing pent-up steam from a pressure cooker.

Holding his hat to his chest, Otha Lee searched each passenger's face as he or she disembarked. Finally, he spotted Otis. Tall, lanky, smooth almond skin, black-framed glasses, wearing a white shirt turned back at the cuffs and gray pants, carrying a briefcase. Otha Lee couldn't help but think what all the white folks on the other platform must be wondering about this spectacular Negro who was walking straight toward him.

"Are you Otha Lee Sturgis?" His voice was smooth, unaccented. He extended a slender hand, which Otha Lee took between his arthritis-gnarled fingers.

"Yes, I am. Welcome home, Otis."

They stood for several seconds, staring into one another's eyes until Otha Lee broke into a huge grin.

"Son, I never thought I'd see you again. And I thought if I did see you, I didn't know you'd be looking so citified."

Otis laughed softly. "You don't suppose I'll stick out too much," he said, surveying the overalled and barefoot peers that milled around the platform.

"Son, I hope you do. We need a little shaking up around here."

"I don't know about shaking up," he said, turning toward Otha Lee. "I hope I'm not putting you out. I can always stay in a motel."

Otha Lee sniffed. "Ain't no motel 'round here for twenty miles that'll take in coloreds. It's me or camp in the woods and hope nobody mistakes you for supper and shoots you."

"I guess I'm staying with you then."

Otha Lee reached for Otis's suitcase and grunted at its weight. "Goodness gracious, what you got in there, son? You bring me a new car from Detroit piece-by-piece?"

"Nothing so spectacular." He lifted the suitcase easily and placed it in the bed of the truck. "Just some books I need to help me with my research and a small typewriter."

Otha Lee wondered how much racket a typewriter created before remembering that he himself snored. "You ready to go?"

"Ready as I'll ever be."

They climbed in the truck. Otha Lee drove slowly past his congregants, letting everyone get a good look at this big city boy who had come to visit. He noticed Otis studying everyone closely.

"Something wrong?"

Otis smiled quickly. "No. I just didn't expect everyone to look so . . ."

"Poor?"

"Not poor. Beaten. As if life has stepped on them like they were bugs."

Otha Lee looked around. He wondered if he and the boy—the man—were seeing the same people. Otha Lee saw people who worked hard but who also played hard, prayed hard, and worshiped hard.

"Maybe. It's Saturday. They been working hard all week in the 'bacca fields and warehouses. Wait 'til tomorrow, after church time. That's when the Spirit revives."

"The Spirit?" Otis's brow wrinkled.

"The Holy Spirit!" Otha Lee laughed, looking back and forth from the road to his son. "You know—the Father, the Son, the Holy Spirit?"

"Oh, yes. I had forgotten."

Otha Lee squinted against the sun and thought a moment before answering. "You forgot the Holy Spirit? Son, when's the last time you been to church?"

Otis shrugged. "I don't know. When I was ten. Twelve, maybe."

Otha Lee slammed on the brakes, throwing them both forward. Otis braced his arm against the dash.

"You telling me you're thirty-seven years old, and you ain't been to church since you was twelve? Since you was a boy?"

Otis threw up hands. "What's the big deal?"

Otha Lee prayed silently. "Dear Lord, they done raised my boy to be a heathen." He took a deep breath. "Son, we going to be doing a lot more than research the rest of this summer."

ten

As Peggy stood at Eva's door, she suddenly remembered a day from their youth. They were all running around the backyard, playing Pin the Tail on the Donkey. It was a brilliant spring day, the twins' birthday. The girls and their brother ran and laughed and played; there was no fussing or fighting or fuming or ordering around. Their parents sat on the wicker love seat, holding hands and smiling, laughing as the five children piled onto them in a heap, overturning the fragile furniture. They took turns churning ice cream, sharing the tasting spoon, getting chocolate frosting from the birthday cake all over their matching blue sailor suits.

Peggy stared at the door until the memory faded. She wondered if anyone else remembered a time when no one could have imagined the day when they would barely speak, and then only in wrath and vengeance and disagreement.

The maid, Delia, appeared and led her to the dining room. Delia had been their parents' maid and went to work for Eva after their mother's passing. Peggy had decided not to employ any of the family's former servants, feeling a need to set herself and these hardworking people free. But all had gone to work for the other sisters, carrying out their duties silently, proudly, but also sadly, Peggy thought. She knew her sisters did not possess their parents' compassion. Sicknesses and deaths among the servants' families went unacknowledged, except by Peggy, who often heard in roundabout ways at the market or the library.

Peggy followed Delia through the shadowy halls into the massive dining hall—to call it a dining room would be an understatement. Imposing breakfronts and china cabinets lined the walls, filled with services for twenty, passed down through the family's various branches since before the Civil War. The family's home had escaped Sherman's fires, as had their extensive holdings and possessions. Mr. Nickles' prudent asset management and his foresighted entry into the realm of manufacturing, a departure from the family's plantation past, had further enhanced the family fortunes. The brothers-in-law had continued the company's expansion into four Southern states, and Eva reigned proudly over the social aspects of this expansion.

The dining table, at least twenty-four feet long, was the frequent scene of society dinners and company business banquets for visiting executives. Eva sat at the head of the table, being served by Leodocia, the kitchen maid. Belva and Beatrice flanked Eva, wearing identical salmon-colored seersucker dresses. The table had been set for only three. Eva spotted her first.

"Why, Peggy! How good of you to join us." Eva placed her palms down on either side of her plate. "Lody, set another place."

"Yes, Miss Eva." Lody went to the buffet table and filled another plate.

"Come and sit down." Eva's voice echoed through the polished hall.

"Peggy, it's so good to see you," Belva said.

"Yes, brunch is not the same without you," said Beatrice, standing and hugging her sister.

Peggy smiled and sat down, placing the linen napkin in her lap. "It's good to know even black sheep can be missed."

Eva studied Peggy, her chin propped on her palm. "And to what do we owe the pleasure of your company?"

"Just being sisterly. Thank you, Lody." The maid set a plate, artfully arranged with fruit, scones, cream, and finger sandwiches before Peggy.

Belva and Beatrice looked at each other, taking deep breaths.

"I also came to tell you that I had Mr. Percy look into it, and he has discovered you have no case or cause to stop work on the church. Work is proceeding." She munched a warm scone, letting it melt on her tongue, savoring Lody's artistry with pastry.

The sisters sat silently.

"Why aren't you eating?" Peggy said, her mouth full. "This is heavenly."

Eva picked up the plate of biscuits Lody had placed next to her. She took four, then passed the plate to Belva.

"Why do you do that?" Peggy said, wiping her mouth.

"Why do I do what?" Eva looked around.

"Take half the biscuits for yourself, then leave the rest for us to divide three ways?"

"The three of you never eat that much. I didn't think you liked biscuits as much as I do."

Belva and Beatrice exchanged a look. "Eva, did you ever stop to think that the reason we eat so little . . ." Belva began.

"Is because you take so much?" Beatrice reached under the table and patted Peggy's hand. Peggy looked down, surprised, realizing that the twins were on her side.

Eva gasped. "I do not take that much. You all make me out to be some kind of pig."

Peggy smiled. "When it comes to biscuits, you are." Belva and Beatrice hid their faces behind their napkins.

"Lody, go get some more biscuits. Apparently my sisters haven't had enough."

"Ain't no more, Miss Eva. Done run out of flour. I'd have to go to the store."

Eva stared at her plate. "Give me that platter, and I'll put some back."

"We don't want them after they've already been on your plate." Peggy picked up a biscuit and buttered it lavishly.

"Now you all make me sound like I'm poisoned."

"Maybe not physically, Eva. But, dear sister, you have a way of eating away at the spirit."

Eva's fork clattered against the plate, echoing through the dark, hot room.

"I will not be spoken to that way in my own home."

"Oh, yes, you will. You are not my mother or my father. You are my sister. Sometimes sisters need to correct one another," Peggy said.

"Correct? You are a fine one to talk about correction. What do you think I've been trying to do with the three of you all these years?"

"Belva, did you know we needed correcting?" said Beatrice.

"No, sister, but now I'm interested to know what's been so wrong with us all these years," Belva replied.

"I don't have to listen to this." Eva pushed back her chair.

"Oh yes, you do. It's about time, too," Peggy said. She walked around the dining room. A soft breeze blowing through the window felt cool against her face. She shot Eva a look from the corner of her eye. "She's jealous of us."

"Jealous?" Eva shook with laughter. "What in the world do I have to be jealous of?"

"Our freedom. Our joy in life and living. Our happiness."

"Need I remind you, Peggy, that your so-called happiness came at a very high cost?"

"Well, at least I earned it."

A fan rattled in the corner. Lody slipped quietly into the kitchen. Peggy thought she probably feared bloodshed.

"Oh, we're back around to that. Peggy the martyr."

"Look around. You got our parents' house. Most of the furniture. Your husband heads the company, and only by the goodness of his heart—certainly not yours—do any of us benefit. You have a beautiful daughter you treat like chattel." Peggy leaned across the table. "Can you look me in the eyes and tell me honestly that having the lion's share of everything makes you happy?"

"Of course I'm happy. And I have freedom, too. Money buys a lot of freedom." She leaned back in her chair wearing a self-satisfied smile.

"What kind of freedom is it, Eva? What have you done with your life? What kind of legacy will you leave Gail?"

"Legacy? Why, she'll have the company."

"I'm not talking about material things. I'm talking about an emotional legacy. A spiritual legacy."

"Gail has attended church all her life. We have given her every advantage, sent her to the finest schools."

"Boarding schools." Peggy spun around. "She's spent more time with nannies and headmasters than she has with her own mother and father. She's lonely. She's lonely in her own family."

Eva stood up. "Is this why you came here today, to point out what you perceive to be my shortcomings? And how dare you tell me how to care for my child? Not that you would know anything about being a mother."

The heavy drapes clung to the wall as if all the air were being sucked out of the room. Peggy heard the echo of a cry in her mind and pushed it away. "I'm not sure why I came. Mostly to see Belva and Beatrice. Maybe the reason I keep coming to these fiascoes is that I keep hoping one day you'll change."

"Since you're such an expert on the subject, please let us in on it. Exactly what do I need to change?"

Peggy grabbed her sister in a tight embrace. She felt Eva stiffen and drew back. "That, for starters. Is it so hard for you to show simple affection?"

Eva's face was hard, her eyes fixed on Peggy's.

"Do you love us? Or are we just another family obligation?"

"Of course I love you." Eva threw down her napkin. "Wherever did you get the idea that I didn't? Haven't I always been there for you?"

"Since when did you ever help us?" Peggy gestured to the twins. "It always seemed like we were the ones who had to help you. Or sacrifice something we wanted for something you wanted. Or give you something of ours because you wanted it, because we had it, or because Mother or Daddy had given it to us."

"I've heard enough. This is so like you, Peggy." Eva placed her hands on her hips. "Pious Peggy. Like you've never done anything wrong. Lody!" she shouted. Lody burst through the door, her eyes darting between the sisters. "Clear the table. Lunch is over." Eva marched from the room, pausing at the door. "If the three of you want to continue this, you may. I have no further use for these pointless arguments."

Peggy and the twins gathered their purses and hurried out the front door. The twins eyed each other nervously before Belva spoke.

"Peggy, are you sure that was a good idea?"

"To make her cut herself off like that?" said Beatrice.

"I couldn't hold it in anymore. Don't you agree that what I said was true?"

"Well," Beatrice hesitated.

"Absolutely," Belva concluded.

"Then it's settled. She never really wanted us anyway. We won't have to make her blasted biscuits anymore."

"That does have its attraction," Belva said.

"Then I'll see you at my house in two weeks." Peggy got into her car and drove away.

Beatrice watched her drive away and sighed.

"What is it, sister?" Belva touched her twin lightly on the arm.

"Actually, I think I might miss the biscuits," Beatrice said, as her sister nodded in sad agreement.

Joseph dropped the hammer into his tool belt and descended from the ladder. Otha Lee was sitting on a stack of lumber talking to himself again. He had yet to bring his son to the church, but ever since Otis's arrival, Otha Lee seemed distracted, almost disturbed. Joseph wondered if he should alert Peggy to the contingency of another drunken episode.

"Joseph, do you believe in the Holy Spirit?"

Joseph dropped the two-by-four he was carrying, startled at the boom in the old man's voice.

"I swear," Joseph said, retrieving the board. "You needing some practice with your preaching voice?" He started back up the ladder.

"I'm serious, son. Do you believe in the Holy Spirit?"

Joseph sighed. Between Otha Lee and Peggy, he had had more theological discussions in the past three months than in his whole life before coming to Bonham.

"I guess so. It's my understanding that the Father, Son, and Holy Spirit are kind of a package deal."

"So they are." Otha Lee went back to mumbling to himself.

"Otha Lee, is something bothering you?"

"You might say that." He got up and handed Joseph another plank. "It's Otis."

"How's he doing? I ain't heard you say much about him since he got here."

"Probably because I'm still trying to figure him out. Hard to explain something to folks you don't understand yourself."

"I thought you said he came down here to do research."

"Oh, he's doing that. Goes to town and interviews them that'll talk."

"What's he interviewing them about?"

"I don't really know. He comes home every evening with a pile of notes and starts clacking away on his typewriting machine. Thing sounds like corn popping over an open flame."

"Does he talk to you much?"

Otha Lee rubbed his chin. "Yeah, but I don't understand half of it. He's pretty citified, you know."

"Yeah. Living in the city makes folks different from us bumpkins."

They walked to the shade tree and gulped large swallows of water. "What was that Holy Spirit question a while ago? That got something to do with Otis?"

"I mean. May the Lord have mercy on my son, but he ain't been to church since he was twelve years old." Otha Lee let the thought hang there for a few minutes while they mopped sweat and hoped for a breeze to kick up.

"I ain't been much of a churchgoer myself, but I have shadowed the door of a few churches since then."

"I just can't understand it," Otha Lee said as if he hadn't heard Joseph speak. "How do parents raise a child without seeing to his spiritual needs? I can't figure that one out. They were good church folks when they were here."

"Maybe church isn't as big a part of life in Detroit the way it is here. What's Otis's explanation?"

"I'm afraid to ask." Otha Lee paced the length of the church. "Now I know in some ways he's a better man than he'd a been if I had raised him. He surely wouldn't've never went to college and became a big professor clacking away on a typewriting machine. But you know something, Joseph?"

"What's that, Otha Lee?"

"He sure would have gone to church. He would've been moved by the Spirit and filled with the Spirit and seen the light of the Holy Spirit of God in Christ Jesus. Amen!"

Joseph laughed. "Speaking of spirits, here comes an earthly one."

Peggy pulled up next to the church and swung out of the car, her dress and hair looking fresh in the wilting humidity. "How's it coming?"

"It's coming, Miss Peggy. I don't know how exactly, but it's coming."

Peggy patted Otha Lee on the shoulder and looked up at Joseph. "How soon do you think it will be ready for a tour?"

"You planning to sell tickets?" Joseph wiped his face with his T-shirt before he realized he had exposed his bare chest.

"Oh, no." She laughed, covering her mouth with her hand. "My sisters," she said, suddenly serious again. "My sisters are coming in a couple of weeks for lunch, and I want to show them around."

"Miss Eva's coming here?" Otha Lee had a strange expression that neither Joseph nor Peggy had seen before.

"No, Otha Lee. Eva's not, but the twins are."

"Does this mean you've got your little land problem worked out?" Joseph lowered his voice as Otha Lee went looking for sandpaper.

"For the time being. My lawyer says Eva doesn't have a case. And the twins were just going along with Eva. You kind of have to know Eva to understand."

"Well, that's good. Say, has Otha Lee said anything to you about Otis?"

"Not much, and I'm about to die of curiosity. Did he come by?"

"No. I never laid eyes on him. From what Otha Lee says, they might not be hitting it off too good."

"I hate to hear that."

"I was thinking maybe we ought to invite Otha Lee and Otis to supper some night."

Peggy regarded him warily. "We?"

"Now hear me out. You know they ain't long on cooking facilities at the boardinghouse, and amazingly I do know my way around the kitchen."

"A man who cooks." Peggy gazed at him appreciatively. "That could be useful."

"In your kitchen it probably could be," he teased.

"Ha, ha. What have you got in mind?"

"If you supply the food, I'll cook, and we can have a supper. Kind of like a dinner party. A welcome home to-do for Otis."

Peggy thought for a minute. "It could be risky. We don't know how comfortable Otis would be with us."

"Are you sure you ain't thinking it might be the other way around? You're used to Otha Lee, but Otis is one of them college professor types. An educated colored. That's something you don't see much around here. It's about as rare as educated whites."

Peggy leaned against the hood of the car, but jumped away quickly, burned by the steaming sheet metal.

"You okay?" Joseph grabbed her arm.

"Yes. I just wasn't thinking about the heat." She gently pulled away.

"Hard to do these days." Joseph looked toward the church. "Let me know what you decide about the supper. We'll try to clean up things a little so your sisters don't fall and break their necks."

Peggy went into the house and changed into her graveyard clothes. The clothes were full of thread pulls, picks, and rips from the thick underbrush that she fought each day. Outside, she grabbed her gloves along with the hoe, rake, and wheelbarrow and set out for her next target, a cluster of six graves that seemed to make up a family plot. The monuments towered over that particular corner of the cemetery. Peggy always believed that such overblown monuments were a waste of money. They were mostly stone obelisks, granite or marble, with little writing, and what there was paid little tribute to the dearly departed. Peggy speculated the size of the statue was supposed to compensate for the lack of sentiment, that a show of money was supposed to atone for a lack of heart.

Peggy brought down the hoe, which clanged against the corner of a flat granite slab, chipping off a small piece of stone. She leaned the hoe against a nearby oak and began pulling at the vines with the rake, clipping them with hedge trimmers and piling them into the wheelbarrow as she went. Sweat trickled down her back and neck; she began itching furiously.

Slowly, she uncovered the slab. Peggy had heard the name before. Alicia Whitfield Nickles, her paternal great-grandmother. The slab contained a lengthy monologue attesting to her womanly, motherly, wifely, and Christian virtues and listed the names of her eight children. Peggy read the names, rolling them over in her memory, trying to place them in the larger scheme of the family's legacy. Other than the testament, the gravestone revealed little of use other than names and dates.

Moving on, she discovered a second slab, equal in size and stone to the first. Patrick Reynolds Nickles, her paternal great-grandfather. By all accounts he was a man of great ambition and forward sight, having managed to save the family fortunes from what the town elders still called "The Late Unpleasantness." He had saved and built and projected and left all of his children handsomely well-off.

He had also left another legacy: slave descendants. More than one hundred slaves had occupied the Nickles plantations at one time. Their descendants populated the county's back roads and the city's back streets. Peggy knew some of them, for they and their parents had continued to work for the Nickles after Emancipation. Yet many were unknown to Peggy because she really did not wish to know. It ached in her heart to know that the family fortunes had been built through the blood and sweat of other human beings who had been bought and paid for like a plot of land or a brood sow. Her family never discussed the subject, and Peggy didn't ask. She had learned enough by accident.

Sitting on a tree stump, Peggy studied the markers, a contrast in sentiments. Alicia's a paean to womanhood, Patrick's an homage to the man who built the church. A tribute to his contribution but not a word about his soul. She pondered the stones for a while as she cooled off. At the Judgment Day, how does one account for owning other people? Is there justification, forgiveness, grace for that?

After dumping the wheelbarrow at the trash heap, Peggy attacked the tangle obscuring the other graves. One by one, she revealed small markers, each with only a name, a date of birth, and a date of death. Three boys, one girl. All dead before the age of six months.

She stared, disbelieving, feeling a sudden headache pull at her temples. She flashed on the funerals of Belva's and Beatrice's infants and grabbed her stomach.

"You need some help?" Joseph leaned against the obelisk, his hands in his dungaree pockets.

"No, I'm about ready to stop." She unclenched her fingers. "Come here and look at something."

Joseph knelt and examined the slabs. "These some kin of yours?"

"My great-grandparents. Look over here."

He hunkered down and ran his hand over a tiny marker. "Died young, didn't they? Didn't hardly even have a chance to live," he whispered.

Peggy nodded.

"You know, lots of babies died back then, Peggy. Doctoring wasn't as good as it is now."

"I know. It's just that I never knew about this."

"Probably some kind of epidemic or something like that."

Peggy read the inscriptions, praying silently.

"You all right? You look like you seen a ghost."

"Do I?" Her hands went to her face. "I think I've just been out here in the heat too long. I need to go inside."

"You want me to go with you? I wouldn't want you passing out from a heat stroke."

"No, Joseph, but thank you." She looked up and smiled. "It was just sad to see, that's all."

"Okay." He turned to leave. "Hey, did you think about what I asked you? About Otha Lee and Otis?"

"Yes, I did. Invite them over Friday night. I know a few people I'll invite, too. We'll make a party out of it. I just hope your cooking lives up to its advance publicity."

"Ma'am," Joseph winked, bowing at the waist, "you are in for a culinary treat."

eleven

Otha Lee sat on the front porch, ventilating himself with a cardboard fan saved from the last funeral he had preached. Otis was inside, getting ready for the supper and playing blues records on a secondhand turntable. The music disturbed Otha Lee. Too much singing about subjects folks ought not to be singing about.

"Otis, get a move on. We going to be late," he shouted through the screened window of Otis's room.

"Be out in a minute," came the muffled reply.

Otha Lee paced back and forth. He knew Joseph and Peggy were sincere, but he wasn't too sure about how Otis was going to act. Forget the fact that Otis was a grown man; he did not always show the proper respect to people, despite who they were. Although Otis had not met Peggy, he already regarded her as some sort of slave master.

Otis came out, dressed in suit pants and a white shirt open at the collar. The intense heat wave showed little sign of abating, and everyone had dispensed with wearing ties for the duration. He checked his watch and snapped it shut, sniffing the night air like a cat sensing trouble. Thunder rumbled from the distance.

"At least somebody's getting rain," Otha Lee said, surveying the stunted cotton field across the road.

"I don't know how you stand it out here." Otis jangled the change in his pocket.

"What do you mean?"

"The silence."

"Silence?" Otha Lee chuckled. "If you think this is silent country, then you ain't listening."

Neither man spoke for several minutes. A lightning bug blinked in the heavy air, and crickets chirped steadily in the woods. A mourning dove cooed in the distance.

Otis took out his pipe and began filling it.

"Son, we ain't got time for smokes. Miss Peggy'll be waiting on us."

"We have plenty of time, Pops." Otis had taken to calling him Pops. He had tried Daddy and Papa and even Dad and Father, but none worked. Otha Lee didn't care for his son calling him by his first name at all, something Otis had also tried. It seemed more disrespectful than the agreed-upon Pops.

"I want to ask you something." Otis rocked back and forth in the freshly painted chair. "Why did this Peggy pick you to give the church to? I mean there has to be some white man of the cloth who is without an abode for his flock."

Otha Lee shrugged, then brightened. "Because she was the way God answered my prayer."

"You prayed to preach at a white man's church?"

"No, no. I prayed for a church building. You saw where the church meets now. Ain't nothing but a bunch of snaky-looking bushes and branches. I need a place where folks can worship the Lord and not get assaulted by wasps and yellow jackets."

Otis puffed and chewed the end of his pipe. "So you're saying that she is just doing this out of the goodness of her heart."

"Yes, I am. And a very good heart it is."

"I did not know anybody in this backwoods place had even heard anything about civil rights."

"We might be in backwoods South Carolina, but we ain't on the moon. We do have radio and newspapers. Miss Peggy's even got one of them television sets."

"You mean you have been in her house before?"

"Yes, when I helped her move in."

"But you have not been inside since then?"

"Unless you count the back porch."

"Not the front porch, just the back porch for us—"

"Don't you use that word. Miss Peggy doesn't treat us that way. Miss Peggy's different."

"Oh, really." Otis blew smoke into the hazy air.

"Most folks won't even allow us in their yard." He shot Otis a bemused expression. "You sure ain't from around here, are you, son?"

"Not since I was born."

Otis tamped out the pipe and stuck it in his pocket with the pouch of tobacco. They climbed into the truck, silent, listening to the growing rolls of thunder that grew closer with each passing mile.

Joseph stood in Peggy's kitchen, a towel slung over his shoulder. The smells of frying chicken and okra filled the cramped room. Peggy sat at the oilcloth-covered table, slicing cucumbers and tomatoes.

"What did you do to that chicken to make it smell so heavenly?" She sat back and inhaled deeply.

"Secret family recipe."

"Family? I didn't know you had one. I never heard you mention one, anyway."

Joseph winced at his slip and turned his attention back to the sizzling pan. He had managed to avoid the subject of family so far.

"Everybody's got family, you know. It's just some families are worth talking about more than others."

"Don't I know." Peggy gathered the peelings and placed them to one side. "Seriously, don't you have anyone? Parents, sisters?"

"No, no one. At least nobody I want to see just yet."

"You make it sound like it's been a while."

"You could say that." He peered into a pot of simmering peas and turned off the rice. "Everything's about ready. Are you?"

"As ready as I'll ever be, I suppose."

Roxie walked into the kitchen, followed closely by a man who seemed to want to stay in the shadows. "Hey, Peggy, what smells so good?" She stopped short and gave Joseph an up-and-down look that made him turn toward the stove and Peggy blush. Peggy grabbed Roxie by the arm and shook her slightly, glaring into her eyes.

"Joseph, this is my friend, Roxie, and this is her friend, um . . ."

"Lester. Lester Quail, ma'am." He extended his hand to Peggy, then Joseph. "Good to make y'all's acquaintance."

"Come on in, Lester, make yourself at home," Joseph said, fixing the newcomer a glass of tea as Peggy and Roxie went into the dining room.

"Very attractive," Roxie said, nibbling on a cucumber.

"Very un-your type," Peggy whispered, glancing at Lester.

"Very change of pace. I'm looking to settle down again." Roxie grinned. "Getting tired of running up and down the road with every Tom, Dick, and Harry. Thought I'd try out a Lester this time."

Peggy laughed, then noticed the time. "He won't have a problem with Otha Lee and Otis, will he?"

"No, not at all. He's so shy he probably won't say a word all night."

"Don't tell me that. That's why I invited you, so we would have talkers."

"Anybody else coming?" Roxie examined her manicure and felt her hair for stray strands.

"I told Gail she could come, but I don't know if she can get away from Eva."

"That child ought to come live with you. At least she might feel like somebody loved her then."

Peggy nodded. She had run into Gail on the street in town. While the camp had not been the disastrous experience Gail expected, she had been homesick and her letters home went unacknowledged by Eva and Gail's father. Gail said she had tied Peggy's letters together with ribbon and saved them in a cigar box under her bed. Peggy had told Gail about the little gathering she was going to have—her niece replied that her parents were going to a party that night, too, and maybe she could sneak away, get Zeke to drive her out.

Otha Lee's truck rumbled into the yard. Joseph went out to greet them while Peggy and her friends stood inside the screened front porch, fanning themselves.

Otis and Otha Lee got out. "Joseph, my friend, I want you to meet my son, Otis."

Joseph held out his hand and was surprised by the professor's strong grip. "I didn't know carrying books around built up so many muscles."

Otis chuckled. "I recommend Shakespeare. He really builds the biceps and the forearms."

They walked onto the porch, and Otha Lee introduced the others. Otis's gaze was penetrating as he shook Peggy's hand, but she met it equally, then withdrew her hand. "Joseph has cooked up quite a feast. Please, come in." She gestured toward the dining room.

Otis and Otha Lee took chairs on one side of the table as Roxie and Lester took the opposite side. Peggy and Joseph brought the steaming platters of food to the table, then seated themselves at the ends. The fan rattled in the corner, lifting the edge of the tablecloth with each oscillation.

"My, my, Joseph," Otha Lee said, breathing in the delicious aromas. "The Lord has blessed you with many talents."

"And we should all be glad," Peggy said, spreading a napkin on her lap.

"What she's saying is be glad I did the cooking instead of her," said Joseph, whose remark was greeted with nervous laughter.

"Otha Lee, would you say grace?" Peggy folded her hands on the table.

"Certainly, Miss Peggy." He bowed his head. "Dear heavenly Father, we ask your blessings on this food and this company, on these friends and on my son, that we may all grow in your light and live according to your will. In Jesus' name, Amen."

"Amen," whispered everyone except Otis. Otha Lee noticed his son did not echo the conclusion.

"Everybody grab what's closest and pass it around," Joseph proclaimed, heaping rice on his plate.

"Otis, how are you enjoying your stay here?" Roxie asked, examining the chicken platter closely and choosing a plump thigh.

"It is quite a change from Detroit."

"I can imagine. Large cities have a life all their own." She sighed. "I really should have been born in a big city. A place like Bonham just isn't big enough for me."

"She means she's too big for a place like Bonham," Peggy said mischievously. She turned to Otis. "Ignore us. We're just messing around like usual."

Otis raised a palm. "On the contrary, I am finding life here quite enlightening."

"Otha Lee says you're a professor," Joseph said, as Lester handed him the bowl of okra.

"That is correct. I teach history at the collegiate level."

"Wasn't one of my strong subjects in school," Joseph said. Everyone else nodded in agreement.

"Otis is writing a book," Otha Lee said, beaming at his son.

"Researching a book, Pops. I won't know until I gather all my information if there is a book there or not."

"What's your subject?" Peggy asked.

Otis picked at his food for a second, then locked eyes with Peggy. "I'm not sure you or your guests would be interested."

Joseph looked back and forth, chewing rapidly. "How can she know if she's interested until you tell her."

"I'm interested," said Lester, his quiet voice startling the company. He shrugged and blushed. "I'm on a kind of self-improvement program. You know, reading books and stuff. Trying to make my mind better." Roxie rubbed his shoulder and beamed, causing him to blush all over again.

Otis's eyes shifted. "I just think some of you might find it disturbing. Particularly a woman like Peggy."

Peggy blinked. "A woman like me? What's that mean?"

"Caucasian. Rich. Upper class. Southern, from a landed family."

"Otis!" Otha Lee stopped eating and glared at Otis.

Peggy smiled thinly. "Well, don't hold back, Otis. Pray tell us what this tome's to be about. My curiosity's been raised."

"The aftermath of slavery and its effects on slave descendants who continue to live near the descendants of their former owners."

The clank of silverware filled the air as a nearing rumble of thunder rattled the windowpanes.

"I thought you said it was going to be about the lives of coloreds in the modern South," Otha Lee said quietly.

"It is."

"That ain't what you just said."

Joseph bent his head over his plate and gnawed a chicken leg to the bone. Lester pushed food around his plate while Roxie studied Peggy out of the corner of her eye. Joseph began to feel this evening had been a mistake. He should never have asked Peggy to do this. Maybe he should have left it all alone.

Peggy wiped the corner of her mouth. "So what are you finding out, Otis?"

Otis laid down his fork and slid his chair back, draping his arm across the back of Otha Lee's. "Many things, Miss Nickles. Many things."

Otha Lee, like Joseph, continued shoveling in food, hoping the sounds of his own chewing would block out anything unseemly he might hear.

"Please, Otis, enlighten us. More tea, anyone?" Peggy asked. Joseph, Otha Lee, Roxie, and Lester held their glasses toward her.

Otis cleared his throat. "For example, the descendants of slaves often still work for descendants of their masters. At slave wages, of course."

"Really. I thought slaves didn't receive any wages. But do go on, Otis."

"Only through oral tradition has any semblance of our African ancestry and tribal customs been maintained."

Joseph lifted his head and studied Otis's and Peggy's faces. There was a sameness to their expressions.

"Fascinating," Peggy replied. "And this figures into your book how?" She got up from the table and began cutting slices of pound cake at the sideboard, arranging them on a china platter and handing it to Roxie.

"Racial identity. The Negro experience in America has been largely co-opted by the white man's desire and need for subservience in order to maintain economic superiority. In essence, greed has taken precedence over humanity."

Joseph looked around nervously, noticing Otha Lee's uncharacteristic silence. "Didn't slavery end a long time ago? I mean, that's what the War between the States accomplished, didn't it?" He felt a little out of his league, not having much of a history background.

"Physically, yes. Unless you count lynchings."

"That doesn't go on here." Peggy's eyes flashed.

"It doesn't go on or you do not hear about it going on—Miss Peggy." Otis speared a piece of cake with his fork.

"Otis, that is enough!" Otha Lee stood and threw down his napkin. "I have listened to you insult Miss Peggy and her friends until I'm just about sick on this fine meal they've prepared."

"She asked me a few questions. All I did was answer them." Otis sipped tea as coolly as if he were attending a faculty reception.

"Well, there are better ways to answer." Otha Lee pushed back from the table and headed toward the door. "Come on. We're going."

"Otha Lee, it's fine. Please don't be upset." Peggy ran after him, leaving Joseph and Otis staring at one another across the table and Roxie and Lester with their eyes glued to dessert.

"Otis, you sure got some strong opinions going for you there." Joseph served himself a second helping of pound cake.

"Not opinions, Joseph. Facts." Otis walked to the doorway. "Just to show I do not lack all the social graces, please give my apologies to Miss Peggy, and thank you for the fine meal. Best I have tasted since I've been here."

"Thanks for the compliment, but I think you should apologize to Peggy yourself. And your pa."

"My pa? He might be the parent of my birth, but he is certainly not my pa."

"Then why'd you come back here? Just to give him a hard time for doing what he thought was best for you?"

Otis was silent. "It was nice to meet you Joseph. Roxie, Lester." He nodded toward the other guests who simply waved. After letting the screen door slam, Joseph noticed that Otis passed Peggy in the yard without speaking. She came in and threw herself on the sofa. Roxie and Lester came in and said it was probably time they left, too, as they were planning to go visit Lester's mother.

"I'm glad you came, although I can't say I'm very glad about how it turned out," Peggy said, rubbing her eyes. Roxie came over and hugged her and patted Joseph on the arm.

"Y'all were just trying to be hospitable," she said, Lester nodding in agreement as he shook Joseph's hand, then went out. "I'll call you next week."

"Joseph, what is it about me that provokes people so? Please tell me. Is it something about my face or my voice? Is it my attitude somehow?"

Joseph studied Peggy for several moments. The hazel eyes, the long hair, the wisps framing her confused but determined face. He sat beside her and took her hand.

"It's not you, Peggy. It's the way the world is now. Everything we used to think was true about people is turning out to be something else."

"Like what?" Peggy said quietly, her fingers folding gently around Joseph's calloused hand.

"I don't know. It's like when you're dreaming and you're in a place that's so real, you think you're in a world that's maybe your real life. Then you wake up and the room is full of moonlight. The curtains are waving in the breeze, making shadows on the ceiling, and you know your body is feeling something your dreaming body never feels. Real life."

Peggy reached up and pushed a curl from his forehead. "I didn't know I was getting a philosopher in the bargain here."

Joseph shrugged. "Maybe I've just had too much time to think." He gestured toward the kitchen. "I better help you clean up in here."

"Don't worry about it. You did all the cooking." Peggy walked him to the door. Lightning flashed brighter. "You'd better get back to town before the storm hits."

"Peggy, I'm really sorry for this evening. . . ." She put a finger to his lips. He took her hand in his and gently pressed his lips against her palm before pulling her into his arms. She pushed away and Joseph saw a tear slip down her cheek.

"No," he said, brushing it away. "We were both trying to do something good for Otha Lee. We just didn't know what we were getting ourselves into."

"I reckon not," she said, grasping his hand. He let go, walked down the steps, and slung a leg over his motorcycle.

"Joseph?" Peggy was backlit, and he could barely make out her face.

"Yeah?"

"Would you like to meet me at church Sunday morning? Just the worship service at eleven. I'm afraid our Sunday school teacher's not that good."

"I don't know. It's been a while since I been to church."

"Think about it. I would like it a lot if you would sit with me."

Joseph smiled as the approaching lightning illuminated the sky, still feeling the warmth of Peggy's embrace. "Maybe it is time I went back."

Otha Lee sat on his bed, staring at the sepia photograph of his wife. A dim bulb hanging from the ceiling scarcely clarified the image.

"I should never have let him go," he said aloud. "He's a stranger to me. I don't understand him, and he understands me even less."

He placed the photo carefully on the nightstand and pulled the string on the light. From the next room, he heard the typewriter clack and a scratchy voice issuing from the turntable's speaker.

"Dear Lord," Otha Lee prayed, falling to his knees. "Please help me find my son. He's not the man I hoped he would be. He's so angry and resentful. He thinks I'm stupid. I know I ain't smart, but sometimes wisdom is more important than knowledge, don't you think? Right now, I'm asking you for the wisdom of Solomon. I don't know how me and Otis are going to find our way back to one another. I know now I was wrong to have given him up. What else could I have done at the time? I couldn't be a father to him in my grief. I missed my wife too much.

"Dear Lord, help me, help us, find our way. Please soften his heart, Father. Help me bring him back to you."

twelve

Peggy sat on the seventh pew from the rear, aisle seat, clutching her purse. She waved politely at a few people she knew and chatted briefly with the usher who handed her a bulletin.

The church seemed unusually full this morning. Peggy heard a baby coo. Looking toward the front of the sanctuary, she noticed two young couples, the mothers holding tiny infants. One of the babies began to cry, and the sound triggered an echo in Peggy's memory.

"Am I late?" Joseph's quiet voice startled her. She slid over, making room.

"Not at all," she said, adjusting her hat and gloves. "You're just in time."

"I think babies are great," Joseph said, following Peggy's gaze. "They haven't got all messed up yet like us old folks."

Peggy noted several stares and covert whispers. It was not the first time she had brought a man to church, but she guessed it must have been a while.

The minister came to the pulpit and raised his hands, indicating for the congregation to stand for the opening hymn.

Joseph took charge of the hymnal, finding the correct page and holding the book open between them. The depth and tone of his voice impressed Peggy. He sang joyfully, barely looking at the words or music. The lady standing in front of them turned and smiled.

Glancing out of the corner of her eye, Peggy quieted her voice to hear his better. Other than playing flute in high school, she had never been very musical herself but appreciated the talent in others. She thought about how often she had heard Joseph whistling as he worked around the church, seeming to hammer in harmony.

The song ended, and everyone bowed their heads for the opening prayer. Peggy stared at the floor for a moment before furtively looking again at Joseph. He seemed so peaceful, at peace with himself. She wished that church made her feel that way. Joseph opened his eyes and looked down at her, smiling. They sat down together, Peggy's arm lightly brushing against Joseph's, and the service proceeded, much of it unnoticed by Peggy.

Joseph took the extended opportunity of the sermon to study the church's interior. It had been a long time since he had been in a real church, one with so much access, not limited by gates and bars and chains.

As he had worked on what had become, at least in his mind, Peggy's church, he felt the place was missing something, an important component that would make it more holy, more sacred. He knew Peggy's windows were going to make a world of difference, but he still felt there had to be more.

Otha Lee had little to say on the subject of aesthetics. At first, he had been so happy just to get the building, all he cared about was having a roof. Now he seemed less concerned with the progress of the church than obsessed with Otis's salvation.

Joseph considered the style of the pews, the windows, the altar, the subtle scent of Peggy's lavender perfume drifting past. He also noticed that her mood had changed considerably as the service progressed. She had strained to see the babies and seemed to take in every detail of their elaborate, frilly dresses. He supposed that Peggy had a baby hunger, like so many other women. He had guessed her to be about his age—mid-thirties— a time when many people were worrying over teenagers, who were worried over cars, clothes, and the opposite sex.

Joseph often wondered why Peggy had never married. She was pretty and very intelligent. It seemed she had read and seen a lot. Yet she held a deep inner sadness that seemed to shadow her, even on days when she seemed happy. Perhaps a trip to the altar could have changed that attitude. Maybe still could.

The altar. Joseph's attention shifted. He studied the altar furnishings meticulously, wishing they were sitting closer to the front, although he had long lost the thread of the minister's droning sermon. The chairs, communion table, and pulpit were very plain, with practically no detail at all.

Just as Peggy held a secret artistic talent, Joseph was a skilled woodworker. He had spent many hours teaching himself the intricacies of carving, sanding, planing, and even design. Woodworking was a skill he had spent many hours finding a way to put to practical use. With his earnings from the church restoration, he had begun to assemble a wide selection of good used tools.

Now he had a plan. He would design and build the new altar furnishings: a communion table, and a pulpit built especially for Otha Lee, one that would reflect Peggy's vision as wrought by the windows, one that would bring the Scripture to life in one more shining way.

He started out of his daydream when Peggy gently tapped him on the shoulder, then slipped her hand into his. The congregation had risen for the final hymn.

Otha Lee and Otis perched on a splintery wooden bench beneath the brush arbor, fanning away the intense heat and a persistent yellow jacket. Otis scribbled furiously in a notebook until Otha Lee whispered viciously in his ear.

"This ain't researching. This is churching!" He snatched the notebook away from his son.

Otis shrugged.

Otha Lee turned his attention back to the service. Since they had suspended him as minister, various elders had taken turns conducting the service. Otha Lee cast a critical ear on their delivery and content and frequently found them lacking.

Today's service was particularly appalling. Roy was leading the service, and he was making a mess of the Sermon on the Mount. Any minister worth his Bible knew that no one ever tried to cover the whole thing in one sermon.

Unlike many ministers, Otha Lee took pride in getting to the point, to the heart of the Scripture. He had tried to stay in practice by rehearsing new material for his son. However, it all seemed to pass Otis by, for all his enhanced education and intellect.

Roy launched into the Beatitudes, reading directly from the Bible. Otha Lee had the entire text memorized. He usually preached without notes and opened his Bible only for effect. The congregation seemed to feel more confident if the minister held the Good Book in his hand. He mouthed along as Roy read but kept his amens to himself.

He looked over at Otis, who seemed to be listening intently. Otha Lee had learned this expression was probably focused more on the delivery than the content. Otis fancied himself something of a public speaker, but Otha Lee longed to give him some pointers on how to emphasize specific points and words to keep his listeners interested, or at the very least, awake.

Otis had treated his father—if it could be called a "treat"— to several examples of his college lectures, attempting to inform him regarding the struggles of their own people. Otha Lee hated to tell him that it was all stuff he already knew because he had lived it, as had his parents and grandparents. The poverty, discrimination, suspicion, fear—Otha Lee had known it all, down to the marrow of his bones.

Roy rambled on. A bee buzzed around Otha Lee's head, and he batted it off, accidentally dislodging Miss Douglas's broad white hat in the process. He also dislodged Miss Douglas. Roy's preaching had lulled her to sleep, and she landed in a heap on the brushed dirt floor. The teenagers on the back row tittered, setting off a wave throughout the assembly. Roy had gone on to the Lord's Prayer and with his eyes closed failed to notice that his congregation was lost. Otis and Otha Lee helped Miss Douglas to her feet and retrieved her hat.

"I'm sorry, Miss Douglas. I was swiping at a bee and wound up swiping you instead," Otha Lee whispered.

"Don't be sorry," she said, her shoulder shaking with laughter as she adjusted her dress. "That man up there's done took away all my joy to the Lord. Ain't nobody even saying amen."

They settled back on their benches. Suddenly Wycliffe stood and faced the congregation.

"Have we all lost our minds?"

Roy's eyes fluttered open, suddenly aware that he was standing before a group of people who were all staring at him as if he were a wad of chewing gum on their shoes. He glared at Wycliffe.

"Brother Wycliffe, have you something to add to the message?"

"Yes, I do." He walked to the front and summoned the other elders to follow. They formed a semicircle around Wycliffe.

"Sit down," Wycliffe said to Roy.

"But I hadn't got to . . ."

"Never mind what you ain't got to. You done been 'round to enough."

"AMEN!" shouted Miss Douglas.

Wycliffe cleared his throat and looked at Otha Lee. "Brother Sturgis, we have done you a grave injustice." The elders nodded in agreement. "We were wrong to suspend you as pastor."

Roy looked around the group. "Who says?"

"We say," said Wycliffe. "The elders had a meeting last week."

"Meeting? Nobody told me," said Roy.

"We decided that we were too quick to judge. All you were trying to do was put a literal roof over our spiritual heads, and we let fear of what *might* be get in the way of what *could* be."

Otha Lee stood slowly and walked toward the elders. "Are you sure?"

"No, we ain't," Roy said, pacing. "Y'all want to go back with a man that's going to get us all lynched?"

"If we are lynched, it will be in the course of pursuing the glory of God." Wycliffe returned to his seat. "Brother Sturgis, will you complete the service?"

Yeses and amens reverberated from the gathering. Otha Lee glanced at Otis, who had begun scribbling in his notebook again. "Yes, I will."

He drew himself up proudly and marched up the aisle, shaking hands along the way. Roy sniffed and stalked out the back.

Otha Lee raised his hands. "Let us pray.

"Dear heavenly Father, we ask your many blessings on this assembly of believers, this gathering of true believers. Let us be witnesses of the faith and carriers of the cause of Christ Jesus. We face many obstacles, Lord, and many trials. But we are grateful for your love and support in our divisions and our togetherness. We ask for your help in bringing your holy Word to this world's unbelievers and the growth of your kingdom. We ask these things in the name of him who died for our sins and ultimate salvation, Jesus Christ. Amen."

The choir stood and broke into song. The congregation joined in, laughing and clapping, in praise and testimony. Otha Lee smiled at Otis, who smiled back, shaking his head as he hesitatingly began to clap along with the worshipers, who were now fully and completely awake.

thirteen

Peggy and the twins sought pockets of shade as they pondered the graves of their dead brothers and sisters, the ones they never knew.

"Did you know about this?" Peggy shielded her eyes against the sun's glare.

"I remember Mother being pregnant when we were little," Belva said. "But when she came back from the hospital, she didn't bring the babies home. Daddy would tell us that the babies had gone to heaven to become angels."

"Yes," Beatrice added, kneeling. "I guess they thought we were too young to handle funerals."

"I wonder why I never knew about this." Peggy sat on a disintegrating stump.

"They probably thought there was no need to mention it," Beatrice said, balancing herself next to Peggy. "After all, you came along and lived."

"Still, one baby doesn't make up for another. We all know that."

Belva and Beatrice had each lost infants, their own flesh and blood, within months of their births.

Peggy was still puzzled. "But why weren't the babies buried in the town cemetery? So they could place flowers."

Belva stroked Peggy's hair. "Sometimes it's easier to forget something when it's not in plain sight. Where you won't run into it all the time."

"Forget it? Why would you want to forget?" Peggy rubbed her arms, feeling a chill in spite of the searing heat. She wheeled and faced her sisters. "Where is *my* baby buried?"

Beatrice went to her. "You mean you don't know?"

"No. I've looked all over the town cemetery. Every cemetery around. I can't find her grave. Or Doug's either."

Belva gently took her arm. "You know that Mother and Daddy took care of everything while you were away."

Peggy laughed quietly and pointed her finger in the air. "I always liked the way you put that—'while you were away.' You mean while I was locked up in a straightjacket, drugged out of my mind. I was already out of my mind. They didn't have to take me out of it further." She ran her fingers through her now-damp hair. "Convenient that my parents died without telling me where they buried my own daughter and husband. Now you won't tell me, either."

"Now, Peggy, listen to me." Beatrice grabbed her by both shoulders. "What is past is past. You are well now. All this anger is not going to bring back your baby or Doug."

"I don't want to bring them back. I just want to put it all to rest."

"Ladies." Joseph had come up, heading for the spigot and a drink of cool water. Otha Lee stood behind him, looking unusually shy.

"Joseph!" Peggy brightened as she introduced her sisters. Otha Lee nodded to each one.

"Still hard to tell you sisters apart. Just like when you was children," he said, holding his hat to his chest.

Belva and Beatrice tittered. "I suppose it does seem silly for us to keep dressing alike," said Belva, "but this way each of us has to make up our mind about clothes only half the time."

They all laughed, then suddenly became silent, instantly aware of where they were standing.

"I hope laughing in a cemetery ain't as bad as whistling past one," Joseph said, breaking the tension.

"Well, I guess we should go in," Peggy said to her sisters, ignoring Joseph's wink. "I've got lunch chilling in the icebox."

Belva hid a smile and nudged Beatrice. "I don't know about you, sister," she whispered, "but I'd say the weather's not the only thing heating up around here."

Joseph and Otha Lee reclined on the church's back steps, eating peanut butter crackers. Joseph pulled a piece of paper from his pocket. It was damp with sweat, but the penciled drawing was still discernable.

"How do you like that?" he said, passing it to Otha Lee, who studied it for several moments.

"A pulpit, if I'm guessing right." He held it away from himself for a different perspective. Joseph pointed to the center of the drawing.

"See there. That's going to be a carving. Moses leading the Israelites out of captivity."

"My son, you *have* been in a church before." Otha Lee laughed and bit off a cracker, spraying crumbs across his shirt.

"I got the idea Sunday when I was in church with Peggy."

Otha Lee's eyes widened. "You and Miss Peggy in church together." He developed a mischievous grin.

"What's that supposed to mean?"

"Nothing. Nothing meant by it at all."

"Anyway, what do you think about the pulpit?"

"I think it's fine, Joseph, just fine. With them fancy windows of Miss Peggy's, I'm 'bout going to have me one of them fancy European cathedrals."

"I don't know about that, but it'll be a sight to behold. I promise you that."

"I can hardly wait now. I got my congregation back. My son's coming along."

"Really? Otis is warming up to the church?"

"Maybe. Finally got him clapping along with the music anyway." Otha Lee brushed the crumbs from his chest.

Joseph chewed thoughtfully. "Sometimes there's a difference between feeling the music and hearing the message."

"Joseph, don't tell me you about to turn into a preaching man, too."

139

Joseph laughed. "Hardly. I don't think they'd give me a license to butcher up the Bible. I think I'll just stick to common sense."

Otha Lee and Otis rocked on the porch, Otis puffing absent-mindedly on his pipe, Otha Lee fanning gnats in the still evening air.

"Tell me about my mother," Otis said quietly, exhaling smoke with each word.

"I thought your Aunt Jolene would have told you all about her. Was her sister, you know."

"I asked her. But it was like she was always too clogged up by grief to tell me anything. All she would say was that my mother was a good woman and let it go at that."

"She was a good woman. Your aunt was right about that."

Otis scooted his chair around to face his father's. "But what was she like? Her personality. Her talents. Her face. Not what she looked like, but what did the world look like through her eyes."

Otha Lee rocked back and forth, his mind searching the past for long-buried images. "She had the soul of an angel. Otis, she loved you before you were born. It was all she wanted in the world, a child. She got down on her knees every morning and every evening and prayed for God to send her a blessing, a child to love and care for." He paused and lowered his head. "She believed in love. She believed in the power of God."

"If she had such strong faith, then why did she die? Why didn't God keep my mother alive?"

"Because we're not in charge. Sometimes God allows things to happen to remind us of who we are and what we are—human. There is a time and a purpose to everything. You'd see that in the Bible if you would open it up sometime."

"What could have been the purpose in taking away my mother?"

Otha Lee raised his head and focused on Otis's eyes in the dim late evening light. He wondered at his educated son, who had rational explanations for everything, who now asked the basic questions of a child. His child. "Look at yourself and who you are now. And look around you. Do you think you could have become the man you are—a college professor, writing an important book—if you had stayed here, raised the son of a hog-raising preacher man in the South Carolina backwoods?"

"Maybe."

"No, son. God had other plans for you."

"Why do you always say God has plans? What about my plans for myself?"

Otha Lee leaned back and laughed. "That's where many folks make their mistakes. Thinking they're in charge of their own life. They forget there's a larger universe at work. A stronger commanding presence."

Otha Lee and Otis listened to the crickets chirp and the faraway coos of mourning doves. At length, Otis went in, and soon the typewriter's clack joined the night chorus, and for once Otha Lee didn't mind the racket.

"Why didn't Mother go to brunch this morning?"

Peggy cringed at the unexpected question. She had settled in for a quiet evening in front of the television when Gail called, upset and worried.

"Honey, it's nothing for you to worry about. Your mother just decided she had other things to do besides listen to my and your aunts' frivolous conversations anymore."

"Does this mean you won't be coming to see me again?"

Peggy caught the sound of impending tears. "Oh, no, not at all." She paused a moment to collect her thoughts. "I'll always be around for you. You know that."

"Then I don't see why you and Mother can't get along. You're sisters, Aunt Peggy. Do you know what I'd give to have a sister? Or a brother? Even if he was a pest?"

Leave it to Gail to insert humor into an otherwise serious moment. "You know how sometimes brothers and sisters—or just sisters—have fights and fall out when they're children? Then they eventually get over it, and before you know what's happened, they're all playing together just like nothing ever happened?"

"Yeah, I guess. Like my friend Melissa and her brother Sam. They fight and make up every day almost."

"Like that. Sometimes people don't get past that even after they grow up. They keep on fighting like children, usually over things that don't make a whit of difference to anyone, not even the ones fighting about it."

"Is that why you and Mother fight? You haven't really grown up yet?"

Peggy couldn't help but laugh. "It's sad but true, sweetie. Don't you worry about me and your mother. We'll make everything right—in time."

"I hope so. Because I'm never going to the beach with her again. I'll go live at camp first."

Peggy took a quick sip of tea and steeled her nerves. "It can't have been that bad."

"Oh, it was." A hard edge stole into her niece's soft voice. "I told you Mother was going to harp at me the whole time, and she did."

Peggy searched for a way to change the subject. The longer they talked about Eva, the more angry she became herself, and it didn't do her niece good to stay perpetually angry with her own mother.

"I'm sorry about that, Gail. If there was anything I could do about it, I would. Maybe by next summer your mother will change her mind and you can come with me on a vacation."

"Where, Aunt Peggy? Where would we go?" The edge left, replaced by a typical twelve-year-old's squeal.

"I don't know. Timbuktu, maybe?"

"Timbuktu? Where in the world is that?"

Peggy burst into laughter. "Why, Gail, it's on the other side!"

At this, they both cracked up, and Peggy vowed that no matter what it took, next summer Gail would be with her.

"I'm going to miss you when I go back to school, Aunt Peggy."

Peggy found her laughter turning into tears. She deplored the thought that Gail would be so far away, but she took a deep breath and tried to smile. "I'm never that far away from you, sweetie." *Because you're always in my heart*, she thought. *Always.*

fourteen

Joseph tried to decide whether he should knock or walk right on in. Once this house had been his home. Now it was simply his mother's house.

Time had not changed the place much. His mother had converted the roof from tin to shingles, but other than that, Joseph saw few differences. Trees he had climbed as a boy were now so tall that a bottom foothold was nowhere within reach. Shrubs climbed over the windowsills, waiting for a long-overdue trim. The old barn sagged under the weight of years.

It was 10:00 Saturday morning. Joseph had risen early, restless, because today was the day he had planned to come home.

He still hadn't told Peggy or Otha Lee. He was beginning to feel close to Peggy, but he hesitated to tell her about his life before Bonham. She had not pressed him, but he often felt she was staring at him in a way designed to divine his thoughts and make the triumphs and tragedies surface like junk through mud after a soaking rain.

Joseph raised his hand to knock, when suddenly his mother snatched the door open.

Zilpha Davidson stared at him as if he were a bandit come to rob her. Joseph opened his mouth to speak, but the words wouldn't come.

They regarded each other for several moments.

"Mama," Joseph said, more as a question, as if to confirm her identity, make sure he had come to the right place.

"As I live and breathe, it's you. Older and grayer, but you all right." She came onto the porch, folded her arms, and cupped her hands under each elbow as if she were cold, although a steamy blue haze filled the air. The screen door slammed shut behind her.

"How are you doing, Mama?" Joseph backed away a couple of steps and stuffed his fingers in his pockets.

"Fine until now. Odd how just about the time you think you've forgotten something or somebody, it all comes popping back up in your face." She stepped forward. "Why are you here?"

"I don't know. I wanted to see you again. See the old house. Make sure you were okay."

"I haven't been okay in twenty years. But I've learned to live with it."

A wasp meandered through the railings, making threatening passes at Joseph. "You need anything, Mama? I mean, I know you still got the truck stop and all, but I'm working a good job and I'd be glad to help you out some here."

Zilpha sniffed and surveyed him up and down, finally resting her eyes on his. "I can't get what I need from you."

"I told you years ago that I'm sorry. I told you I didn't mean to do it. I told the judge and jury that."

"They didn't believe it, either." She sat on an old straight chair prickly with ripped cane and turned her head where he couldn't see her face.

"I told the truth, Mama."

"You never knew what the truth was. All you ever did was lie."

"You ain't got no right calling me a liar." He slapped his hand against a post. "I never lied about what happened that day with me and Brett."

"You killed your brother. Ain't nothing you could ever say or do that can bring him back or convince me otherwise that you didn't murder my son in cold blood."

"I'm your son, too, in case you forgot. Doesn't that count for anything?"

"No, it don't. The truth is you ain't my son." She paused and stared at her feet. "Never were."

Joseph moved toward her. "What're you talking about—'never were.' Of course I'm your son. I was born in this house, wasn't I?" Joseph ran his hands through his hair. "Weren't you there? Wouldn't you remember giving birth to me?"

"I would if I had, but I didn't." She finally looked him in the eyes.

"Well, if you aren't my ma, are you going to tell me next my pa wasn't my pa?"

"No, he was your pa. But Brett was your half-brother."

Joseph sat heavily on another beat-up chair. "So you mean my whole life I was thinking you were hating your own flesh and blood when you were really hating me because I wasn't." His hands balled into fists. "No wonder you were so glad when they hauled me off to prison."

"You killed my son. MY son. That's something that don't bear forgiving."

Getting out of the chair, Joseph took in one last view. "This was surely a big mistake, my coming here today." He jumped off the porch and mounted his motorcycle. "Can I ask you one last thing, and I'll never darken your door again."

Zilpha pulled at the fringe of a rug hanging over the banister. "If you have a need."

"If you ain't my mama, then who is? Or was?"

Zilpha shrugged. "Ask your pa."

Joseph laughed. "Now I'm thinking you must be crazy and all this has been out-of-your head talk."

"Nothing out of my head about it. Ask your pa."

"You wrote and told me he was dead."

"He was dead to me." She dusted off her hands, clapping them together. "He ran off. Don't ask me where; I don't know."

Joseph felt the heat choking him, as if two hands were crushing his windpipe. "Then why would you write and tell me he was dead?"

"Because he might as well have been. Brett's dying—Brett's murder—drove us apart. I knew you killed him, but your pa wouldn't believe it. He went crazy on me. Must be something that runs in your family." She cackled at her attempted joke.

"Get on, now. I got nothing else to say." She went back in the house, the screen door hinges squeaking in the still air.

Joseph jumped on the starter, pushing the motorcycle to life, his mind reeling, finding no direction in the dust that flew around him as he drove away from the only home he had ever known.

Peggy had cleared nearly half the cemetery, and as she exposed each marker, she meditated on each name. She did not recognize most of them, although from time to time, she found friends of her parents or more distant relatives—cousins and maiden aunts and such. The graves were more recent, dating from the turn of the century and into the 1920s. Some tombstones already had surrendered to the ground, felled by storms or vandals. Others were pocked by cracks, dug by rain that had seeped in and frozen, only to leave jagged scars.

No breeze disturbed the sultry air. Puffy, low-lying clouds filled the sky, a sure sign that a tropical storm brewed somewhere in the nearby Atlantic. Only forty miles away, Bonham was subject to occasional swipes from hurricanes and other tropical systems that skirted the coast. It was a rare occurrence for one to come inland or to be so severe as to cause major damage.

A distant roar caught Peggy's attention. Joseph's motorcycle. He came toward her trailing a cloud of dust, skidding to a halt before uncharacteristically letting the machine fall to the ground. Peggy went to him, removing her gloves and wiping sweat that trickled down her neck.

"I didn't expect to see you today, Joseph."

"Didn't expect to find myself here." His voice sounded edgy, angry almost.

"Are you all right?"

Joseph paced around for a minute before hurling himself to the ground. "Did you ever wake up one morning and discover that everything you ever believed about your life up to that point had turned out to be one solid block of lies?"

Peggy contemplated the question as she situated herself next to him on a gnarled root. "I believe I have had that experience several times." She reached over and took his hand. "You seem like a man whose illusions have been shattered."

"Shattered? How can something shatter that never really existed?"

"Such philosophy." Peggy tried catching his eyes, but they were staring at a faraway place. "You want to tell me what's happened?"

Joseph sighed. "I went to see my mama this morning."

Peggy blinked. "You gave the impression you had no family."

"Turns out I was under the impression I did." He looked at Peggy and tried to smile. "Guess I'm not making much sense."

"A little background would be helpful."

"I hadn't seen my mama in many years. I guess you could say we had quite a falling-out."

"How many years?"

"Twenty."

Peggy nodded. "Go on."

"I guess being around this church all the time put me in mind of a reconciliation. Forgiveness and all that. So I decided to go home and try it."

"Only your plan didn't work out."

"You could say that."

"So what did your mama say?"

"Told me she wasn't really my mama."

Peggy sucked in her breath. "You mean they adopted you, and you didn't know about it?"

"In a manner of speaking. Turns out she's not my mama, but my pa really is my pa."

"Is? So I take it he's still alive?"

"I don't really know. She wrote to me years ago telling me he had died. This morning she tells me he run off and left her and she don't know where he is. She doesn't know who my real ma is either."

"Wow."

They sat listening to the breeze that had begun to stir in the treetops. Joseph rested his elbows on his knees. "I don't know if she was telling me the truth about that, either."

"Can I ask you something, Joseph?"

"Yeah."

"What did the two of you fall out about? All those years ago."

Joseph hesitated. Peggy was the first person to trust him in years. The truth hung in his mind and swung like a pendulum. It was bad enough that his life had been blown apart. He couldn't bear to lose anyone else today.

"I can't rightly remember now. You know how you argue with someone and ten minutes later you can't remember one another's exact words, but the anger and the hurt keep on burning like a bonfire somebody's still piling the firewood to?"

"Yes. I think I've had that argument."

Joseph looked around at the cleared spaces. "It's starting to look good out here." He took Peggy's hand and helped her up. "I didn't mean to pour out all my troubles on you." He whistled softly. "Or maybe I did. Why else would I come here straight off?"

Peggy smoothed a stray hair from his forehead. "I owed you one for me dumping on you during our trip to Charleston." Her face brightened as she pulled a letter from her pocket. "The stained-glass people wrote me. The windows will be coming in October."

Joseph blew out air. "I ain't even thought about those things. I don't know that me and Otha Lee can handle them without shattering them to bits."

"Don't worry about that. They're going to send a special crew of men experienced at installing stained glass."

"Good. You had me worried there for a second." They looked toward the church. "It's all going to be all right, ain't it? The church, I mean."

"Yes, Joseph," she said, gazing into his eyes. "It's all going to be all right." She turned and walked toward the house.

"Peggy?" Joseph leaned against the tree.

"Yes?"

"Would you escort me to a movie this evening?"

Peggy smiled. "I would like that, Joseph. Very much."

Peggy went inside and collapsed before the fan. It had been a long time since she had been to a movie with a man. In fact, she couldn't remember when she had been on a date.

Lately her thoughts focused more and more on Joseph. She sensed that he had lost something important, something fundamental, but she did not feel it her place to pry. She decided that Joseph was the type to open up on his own, when he decided the time was appropriate, so she was glad he felt he could trust her enough to tell her what had happened today.

Yet Peggy knew she had a past that needed accounting for as well, and she didn't know where to begin. There were times when she and Joseph were alone, apart from Otha Lee, that she felt a sudden longing to tell Joseph all of her thoughts and dreams, her mistakes and apprehensions. Her fear of ending up alone, the caretaker of a long-abandoned cemetery and a menage of stray feral cats. But she feared he would walk away, like so many men, at any admittance of desperation. When she thought about it, she nearly wanted to abandon herself, to take off and become someone else, someone new, in a new town, a different place, as if you could just change your outfit and become someone new.

She shook her head and rose to draw a bath. It occurred to her that maybe she and Joseph were dating. *Courting* was the old-fashioned word she preferred. Something at once innocent and flirtatious, slow, designed to reveal each other's hearts and souls by degrees rather than by full admittance and exposure.

Peggy remembered that old childhood chant:

> *Peggy and Joseph sittin' in a tree*
> *K-i-s-s-i-n-g.*
> *First comes love, then comes marriage,*
> *Then comes Peggy with a baby carr . . .*

Peggy stopped cold, staring at herself in the bathroom mirror as steam rose from the tub and clouded away the stricken face that had stared back too often to mention.

Joseph and Peggy window-shopped along Main Street, where shopkeepers had filled the windows with back-to-school displays.

"Remember your first day of school?" Peggy said, staring wistfully at a stack of fresh notebooks and pencils in the drugstore window.

"Actually I've tried to forget," Joseph said slyly.

"Don't tell me you didn't like school."

"I wouldn't say I didn't like it. More like it didn't like me." They sat on a sidewalk bench. "I guess I spent too much time fooling around. I'm sort of embarrassed to admit it, but I never finished."

"Oh my. Why not?" Peggy pressed her fingers to her lips. "I'm sorry. I'm prying into your business."

"That's all right. Things happen. It was still the Depression then, you know."

"Oh yes. I had nearly forgotten."

"I bet you were a straight A student."

"Mostly A's. I loved art classes, of course. And I studied and made good grades, but I never found much that really interested me."

"Speaking of art, have you done anything much with that lately? That fella in Charleston felt really strong about you taking up stained-glass designing."

"I don't know about that." Peggy sighed and looked up at the stars. "I have been doing some sketching. I might take up the paintbrush again."

"I wish you would. You have a real talent, Peggy. It's a gift. I'd hate to see you lose it for lack of use."

Peggy smiled. "And what about you, Joseph? The church is going to be finished soon, and I'm afraid you'll be out of a job."

"Been thinking about that." Joseph pulled out his wallet and extracted the drawing of Otha Lee's new pulpit. "I'm thinking of starting a woodworking and furniture repair shop. Maybe even go to making church pulpits for a living."

Peggy examined the drawing, holding it up to the nearby streetlight. "Joseph, this is extraordinary." She folded the drawing carefully, handed it back, and shrugged. "Maybe I could help with the carvings. I have done some sculpting as well."

"I'd like that," Joseph said. "Very much." He looked back and forth along the street. Most of the moviegoers had gone home, and no one moved except a stray white dog that sat on a corner scratching fleas. "Peggy?" Joseph whispered.

Peggy turned to find her face inches away from his, his gaze wandering past her hair as he slid a hand behind her neck. He leaned in and brushed his lips against hers, just enough to set off a tingle down her spine, a feeling she had not sensed in fifteen years. He pulled back.

"Do you want me to . . ."

"Stop? No." She settled into his embrace as they drank in each other's feel and scent in the humid night air. Joseph pulled away slowly.

"It's been a long time since I touched a woman this way. Maybe never," he said, looking sad. "I don't want to hurt you, Peggy. There's a lot you don't know about me."

Peggy took his face in her hands. "You can't hurt me, Joseph." *You can't break what's already been broken*, she thought, as a rushing sound filled her mind.

He stood and held out his hand. "I'd better take you home now."

They walked, holding hands, to his motorcycle. They embraced again in the moonlight, both thinking that tonight their lives had finally turned a corner, but remembering that no one ever turns a corner knowing exactly what lies ahead.

Joseph arrived at work Monday morning to find Otha Lee measuring out pew lengths. Joseph looked around anxiously. "Have you seen Peggy this morning?" Distracted, he grabbed a sheet of plywood, placed it on the sawhorses, and began measuring.

"No. Car's been gone since I got here." Otha Lee examined Joseph's expression. "That is the face of a worried man. One that knows better'n to make pews out of plywood."

Joseph took a deep breath. His heart had been thundering ever since he and Peggy kissed. He had dated a few women right after he got out of prison and was living over in Lexington, but he had never been serious about any of them, and he certainly had never felt about any of them the way he felt about Miss Peggy Nickles.

And that was what worried him. He had not seen her Sunday. In fact, he had intentionally avoided going to church. It wasn't like they had a standing date—it was more like an open invitation. Now, though, he feared seeing her again. Afraid that reality had set in and that she had realized he was just the hired help, someone she knew virtually nothing about, someone afraid of what he felt and how he should show it.

Peggy drove up and emerged from the car carrying a large white paper sack. The air was cool this morning from a light breeze teasing through the pine woods, a slight letup in the ongoing heat wave.

"I thought you fellas might enjoy some fresh doughnuts this morning, straight from the Bonham Bakery." She held the bag out to Otha Lee, then Joseph, whom she lightly brushed against as she lay the bag on the makeshift table. She winked at Joseph, and he exhaled loudly, winking back.

"I'm going to make you two some coffee. Be back in a few minutes."

After she had gone, Otha Lee grinned broadly at Joseph.

"What're you gawking at?" Joseph asked, unable to contain a grin of his own.

"You young people in *love.*" Otha Lee put a special emphasis on the last word, wiping powdered sugar from his lips.

The last word brought Joseph up short. "Who says we're in love?" He turned away so Otha Lee couldn't see his face.

"Your eyes, your mouths, your foreheads. Your arms, your legs. That little wink y'all don't think I saw."

Joseph laughed in spite of himself. "Geez Louise, I reckon we're going to have to start wearing masks if we stay around you."

They passed the bag back and forth until Peggy returned with two steaming cups of strong black coffee. They nodded their thanks, and she retreated to the house, occasionally glancing over her shoulder at Joseph, who was making it a point not to notice.

"I'd think that young lady was sixteen 'stead of thirty-six," Otha Lee joked.

"All right, all right already." Joseph studied the church. "Otha Lee, can I ask you something?"

Otha Lee nodded, chewing rapidly.

"In spite of all your problems, are you glad Otis has come home?"

Otha Lee sipped his coffee carefully. "I thank the Lord every day that I have a second chance with my son. And I ask the Lord to help me find our way back to each other and for Otis to find his way to God."

"Is it working?"

"Is what working?"

"Praying."

"Prayer always works, Joseph. It's just that sometimes the answers we get ain't the answers we want. Is there something bothering you?"

Joseph shrugged. "A few things." He recounted the visit with Zilpha Davidson. "There's other things, too. Things about my life I haven't come clean with Peggy about yet."

"I expect there's a few things Peggy ain't come clean with you about, neither."

"What do you mean, Otha Lee?"

"Oh, all I mean is when two folks are trying as hard as the two of you are to impress one another, each is bound to leave some chapters out of the story."

They left the cups on the stump and resumed their work. Joseph ran his hands across the siding, peeling paint as he went.

"Have you been hearing about them big hurricanes?" Otha Lee scratched his chin.

"Yeah, I been listening to the radio news. They had something about it on the newsreel at the movie the other night." The busted windows would soon be removed. "I was thinking about those stained-glass windows, too. Hate to see 'em get blowed out."

"What you thinking about?"

"Storm shutters. That way if a storm comes before we get the windows, we can protect the inside of the church. If a storm comes after, we can keep the windows safe." Joseph pulled a scrap of paper from his pocket. "I came down here yesterday morning and measured so I could figure up materials."

Otha Lee clapped him on the shoulder. "Joseph, you are a smart man."

"I'll settle for just having good sense," he replied. *And Peggy,* he thought to himself. *For a lifetime.*

Fifteen

The torches cast shadows against the sides of the brush arbor as Otha Lee took a deep breath. A young girl stood on either side of the makeshift pulpit, fanning him with large palmetto fronds, keeping away the gnats and flies and mosquitoes that had begun to make the September air unbearable.

Revival—it was the autumn rite for every self-respecting Southern Negro Christian. A guest speaker had been unavailable, so Otha Lee had taken the responsibility himself. This was the final night, and he was tired in body, but his spirit felt enriched, golden, ready to cast forth his greatest sermon, the one that would draw penance, the one that would convert the unbeliever, convince the saved, and drive home the presence of the Spirit of God in Christ Jesus.

He looked out over the congregation and caught sight of Otis, taking notes again. He felt an anger rise in his belly, then calmed it with a deep breath, saying a silent prayer. "Conversion comes in your time, Lord, not mine. I only ask you this. Could you let it be tonight?" Grasping the sides of the pulpit, he began.

"Paul was a man who liked writing letters. That was his way of getting the word around about this man, this great man, called Jesus Christ."

A few quiet amens came from the assembly.

"He was having trouble, though. He was having trouble making himself understood. Getting people to turn around to the Lord. He had to make himself plain, so they'd understand and take heart. So he wrote a letter to the Corinthians."

Otha Lee took up his Bible and opened it so it would lay spread across his left hand. He looked at it once, for effect, then to Otis, who wasn't paying attention at all, engrossed as he was in his notebook.

"First Corinthians, chapter three, verse ten," he thundered, although no one opened a Bible. Few had one and of those that did, fewer could read well enough to follow the words. "'According to the grace of God which is given unto me, as a wise masterbuilder, I have laid the foundation, and another buildeth thereon. But let every man take heed how he buildeth thereupon.'"

"Amen." Wycliffe nodded to Otha Lee.

"'For other foundation can no man lay than that is laid, which is Jesus Christ. Now if any man build upon this foundation gold, silver, precious stones, wood, hay, stubble; Every man's work shall be made manifest: for the day shall declare it.'"

He paused to gather in the gaze of his congregation and slammed the Bible down on the pulpit, causing Otis to raise his head with a look of curiosity.

"Because it shall be revealed by fire!"

"Amen, brother. Preach on." Miss Douglas stood up and clapped.

"Amen, sister. Paul wrote: 'And the fire shall try every man's work of what sort it is. If any man's work abide which he hath built thereupon, he shall receive a reward.'"

"The Lord is good!" Miss Douglas remained standing and shook Otis's shoulder.

"He is good and merciful, Miss Douglas." Otha Lee took off his glasses and wiped the sweat streaming down his forehead with a dry handkerchief. "But Paul wanted us to know this: 'If any man's work shall be burned, he shall suffer loss: but he himself shall be saved; yet so as by fire.'"

His voice had fallen to a whisper, and the congregation leaned forward to catch the verse. He rubbed his palm across the Bible's cracked leather surface, leaving a trail of sweat. Raising his eyes, he found Otis watching him intently, his pen hanging loosely from his fingers.

"Fire." He walked around the pulpit into the center aisle. The children followed, struggling with their unwieldy fans. "The Lord baptizes us by fire, tries us by fire, tests us by fire." He launched into the next round. "Shadrach."

"Shadrach!"

"Meshach."

"Meshach!"

"Abednego."

"Abednego!"

"Nebuchadnezzar didn't like the answers they gave when he told them to worship his god. A golden image. A pagan god. He didn't like what they had to say. So the Bible says he had them thrown into the midst of a burning fiery furnace."

"Lord help 'em!"

"It was hot in that furnace, hotter'n this heat wave we been suffering through these many weeks. Hotter'n the fire in your stove at home. Fire so hot it burned up the men who put Shadrach, Meshach, and Abednego into the burning fiery furnace."

"Save 'em, Lord, save 'em all."

"He did." Otha grasped Miss Douglas's hand and squeezed it tightly. "The Lord showed his mercy on Shadrach, Meshach, and Abednego. The Lord was on their side. And whose side is the Lord on now?"

"Our side!" The congregation clapped and shouted. Otha Lee glanced at Otis and saw the notebook closed on the bench next to him. He raised his eyes. "Dear Lord," he prayed, "for once he's listening."

He turned his attention back to the congregation. "The Lord spoke to Isaiah, 'When thou passest through the waters, I will be with thee; and through the rivers, they shall not overflow thee; when thou walkest through the fire, thou shalt not be burned; neither shall the flame kindle upon thee.'

"Fire, brothers and sisters. Fire." He pointed to the torches that lit the arbor. "Fire that casts light can also harm. But we can learn from fire. Draw strength from fire. Find love through the fire."

"Preach on, Brother Otha." Miss Douglas rocked back and forth on her bench, fanning herself with an old Bible tract.

"I will, sister. Job."

"Tell it."

"Job was a righteous man, a good man, a rich man. Now, don't you know, friends, that it's easier for one of them old humpbacked desert camels to go through the eye—I said the eye—of a needle than it is for a rich man to enter the kingdom of heaven?"

"Lord have mercy on rich folks." Wycliffe shook his head.

"They need it, brother. So now here was Job sitting up here all righteous and fat and happy with all his young 'uns, and old Satan comes up and tells God he can make Job turn against him. So God up on his throne in heaven says, 'Satan, have at it.'"

"Lord have mercy on us all, the devil's done got loose."

"And still is. Well the devil done come and heaped all kinds of plagues on Job. His servants get killed. His camels get stolen. His children die in a great wind. He gets covered with boils from head to toe. In the middle of all this one of his servants came up and told him the fire of God is fallen from heaven, and hath burned up the sheep, and the servants, and consumed them." He paused and focused on Otis for a second. Otis had propped his chin on his palm and had closed his eyes. Otha Lee strode to Otis's bench and knocked his palm out from under his face, then made his way back to the pulpit.

"Job had many tests. And among them was fire. Can I get a witness?"

"Amen!" came the shouts from the four corners of the arbor. Otis rubbed his chin and started to pick up his notebook, only to lay it down again after a withering stare from Otha Lee.

"Elijah."

"Elijah!"

"Elijah was a man of God, a man of prophecy, a man of great power. He summoned the fires of the Lord to burn up the men who questioned his authority as a man of God.

"So one day the prophet E-lij-ah and the prophet E-lish-a are speaking together. It is the day God has decided to call E-lij-ah home. And how does he come get him?"

"A chariot of fire!" Wycliffe clapped his hands.

"A chariot of fire pulled by horses of fire. The power and the glory of the Lord come down as fire." Otha Lee pulled out his handkerchief and mopped sweat from his chin. The children had given up fanning and sat leaning against their mother on the front bench.

He took a deep breath.

"Moses."

"He gone lead Israel into the Promised Land!" Miss Douglas held up her hands and rocked back and forth on the bench.

"Moses is out yonder in the desert watching his daddy-in-law's sheep." Otha Lee turned to the third chapter of Exodus, verse two, and laid the Bible on the pulpit. "'And the angel of the LORD appeared unto him in a flame of fire out of the midst of a bush: and he looked, and, behold, the bush burned with fire, and the bush was not consumed.'" He looked out at Otis, who had resumed scribbling. "Moses was confused. He couldn't understand. This bush is out here burning, just like we'd burn off a field come winter, but it ain't burning up!" He shook his head and walked back into the aisle, snatching the notebook away from Otis.

"Then he hears the voice of God—and it's calling him from the bush—'Moses! Moses!' And Moses says, 'Here I am.' And God tells Moses who it is calling him from that bush—it's God himself!"

"Hallelujah!" Miss Douglas stood up in praise.

"And God tells Moses he's the God of Abraham."

"Abraham!"

"Isaac."

"Isaac!"

"And Jacob. Praise God."

"And Jacob! Praise God Almighty!"

"He tells Moses he's got a job to do. He's looking down from heaven, and he's seen the troubles of the Israelites. And he's got a place for them to go. A land flowing with milk and honey. And it's gonna be Moses' job to lead them out of Egypt into the Promised Land." He put Otis's notebook on the shelf under the pulpit.

"But Moses is standing there hemming and hawing. He questions God. 'Who am I that I should go unto Pharaoh, and that I should bring forth the children of Israel out of Egypt?' He's scared now, and he's standing there asking, 'Why me? Why me?' And he asks God, 'Well, what should I tell the people your name is? They gonna wanta know!' And God answers—say it with me now—'I AM THAT I AM!' He says, 'Tell 'em I AM sent me.'"

"Glory be!"

"It took a while. Moses had a lot of excuses. He couldn't speak good. The Israelites might laugh at him. Not believe him. He even begged God to pick somebody else. But God finally got good and mad and it finally sunk into Moses' thick head that he was the one—the one God had chosen—to lead the Israelites to the Promised Land.

"And God spoke these things from a burning bush."

"He's gone lead us all into the Promised Land."

"Brother Wycliffe, praise God, you been listening." Otha Lee mopped the sweat dripping into his eyes and rubbed them for a moment. He began again, quietly and purposefully.

"You all know about the fire that took away my family when I was just a boy."

"Amen." The congregation became still.

"It was an awesome blaze. It lit up the night sky for miles around. I stood and watched it from the woods. Was nothing I could do. I had to stand alone and watch my whole family burn up in that unholy blaze." He looked into Otis's eyes. "But even though I was standing alone, brothers and sisters, I wasn't the only one there that night. There were many others." He shook his head. "Many others."

"My daddy was a good man, an honest man, a man trying to improve things for his family and the community. He was a freed slave, a sharecropper. The Nickles family freed him."

A whisper rippled through the congregation.

"But he was working for somebody else, a man that didn't treat folks the way the Nickles did. Didn't treat him fair. Daddy tried to get a fair wage, a fair price for his crops. White folks didn't like this. Said Daddy wasn't staying IN HIS PLACE."

The crowd erupted, arms waving, voices shouting, people standing. "We know what that place is," a man yelled from the back row.

"Yeah, we all know what that means. So they got up a little group. A group of men, all dressed up in white sheets and hoods, hiding their faces. I come up behind 'em. They all standing around laughing, watching my daddy's house, with my daddy and my mama, and my brothers and sisters, inside, burning up." He leaned heavily against the pulpit and wiped the tears from his eyes. "They start pulling them hoods off. One by one their faces come into view. And one of them faces is Mr. Leonard Nickles."

The congregation sat in stunned silence. Otis tilted his head to one side and started to rise from his bench. Otha Lee motioned him back down.

"Son, I ain't done yet. He had a look on his face—a look of horror like I ain't never seen before nor since. He ain't had no idea what them other young fellas was planning. See, he wasn't more than a young 'un himself. Not much older than me. He turned and tried to run away, but the other fellas they caught him and beat him and made him swear an oath that he won't never tell the deed done there that night."

Otha Lee looked at Otis and caught the tightness of his jaw. "I was scared; I ain't gone lie. I thought for sure that once they found out I was still alive that they was gonna come after me, too. But they never did."

He leaned wearily against the pulpit and prayed silently for strength to finish the message. "Seeing all that, I was like Moses. I knew that God had his purpose in me seeing all my family killed. It took me a long time to accept what that was. In his own way, God was calling me through the fire to preach the gospel. To find forgiveness. To walk away from the hands of hate to the blessings of the hands of love."

"God bless you, Brother Otha." Wycliffe began clapping along with the others in the assembly.

Otha Lee held up his hands for silence. "After that night, it seemed like Mr. Leonard made it his special purpose to help me out. He got his daddy to give me a job, and after old Mr. Leonard died, young Mr. Leonard kept me on.

"Now you all know that soon we will be moving into our first real church building. A building given to us by the blessings of Mr. Leonard's daughter, Miss Peggy."

"God bless her," said Miss Douglas. "Amen," came the echoes from the crowd.

"I got no idea that she knows anything about what happened on that night of fire." He sighed. "That night, I could have become an angry man, a man full of hate, full of bitterness. But God showed me that while he can consume by fire, and instruct by fire, he can also cause hearts to change—all by fire. That night, I believe I was chosen to preach the gospel. And Miss Peggy don't know it, but she's finishing something that was started years and years ago. She may not even know her own reasons for buying that church, then giving it to us, but God knows hearts better than we do. Sometimes God chooses a child to atone for the sins of the parent. Mr. Leonard paid his debt to me many years ago. Now Miss Peggy is paying his debt to the heavenly Father. For unto whomsoever much is given, of him shall be much required. Let us pray."

The congregation bowed their heads, save Otis, who stood and stared at Otha Lee for a few seconds before stalking out of the back of the arbor. Otha Lee raised his eyes. "Heavenly Father, we are reluctant to do your will, and we often forget to ask what it might be. Sometimes you have to do drastic things to get our attention. Sometimes you have to send a little fire our way. We ask that you bless this congregation and those who have heard this sermon. We pray that a fire for God the Father, God the Son, and God the Holy Spirit will be set in these hearts tonight. In Jesus' name we pray. Amen."

"Amen."

Otha Lee picked up his Bible and walked through the arbor, shaking hands, looking out the back for Otis. But no matter where he looked Otis could not be found. Otha Lee wondered if he ever would.

sixteen

Peggy and Joseph stood before the nearly completed church as Joseph prepared to take her on a tour. Peggy had scheduled the windows to arrive the next day; it would take the crew about a week to install them. Then they would paint the church, pale blue inside and white outside, and Joseph would finish work on the furnishings, altar pieces, and pulpit.

Peggy grasped Joseph's hand. They had been to church several times and on dates to the movies. She felt they had grown closer, but she still sensed a distance in Joseph, as if there were something he wanted to say but couldn't find a way to bring it up.

As they walked around the sanctuary, examining details, Peggy felt a sudden sense of trepidation. She had longed to see the church completed, but now that the day was drawing near, she worried over its effects. How would the community react to the changeover from white to colored ownership? Was she placing Otha Lee and his congregation in danger?

"Peggy?" Joseph was watching her with a puzzled expression. They were back outside the church now, where he was demonstrating the new storm shutters.

Peggy shook her head. "I was off in a cloud, wasn't I?"

"I'll say, and floating far away from here."

Peggy laughed softly. "I suppose I feel a little like the bride before the wedding—about the church, I mean."

"How's that?"

"I'm afraid for Otha Lee and his congregation. I don't know if I'm doing the right thing by turning the church over to him."

"It's kinda late to be worrying about that now, don't you think?"

"I guess so. I just don't want anyone to get hurt."

"Are you really worrying about them?" Joseph lifted her face, meeting her eyes. "Or are you worrying about the fallout on you?"

"The fallout's already begun. You see how no one speaks to me after church, even when I speak first. It's like all the people I've known my whole life have suddenly become strangers."

Joseph nodded. "I know the feeling."

Peggy searched his face. "You always seem as if you've lost something. A part of yourself." She looked at her feet for a moment. "I'm not talking about your mother. Or the woman you thought was your mother."

Joseph's eyes lingered over the church before meeting Peggy's. "I didn't think I was such a see-through guy." He reached for Peggy's hand. "What I've lost can't be got back. That's the way it is with most things gone for good."

"I know," Peggy said, nodding. "If only there was a way to make time reverse itself."

"I don't know if that would necessarily be a good thing." He pulled her to him. "Then you and me wouldn't be standing here smooching in a spooky old graveyard."

They kissed for several moments, their arms wrapped around each other.

"Turnabout's fair play," Joseph said playfully, smoothing her hair. "Now I want a tour of the boneyard."

"Don't call it that," Peggy scolded, slapping him on the shoulder and shoving him away. "It's sacrilegious." She tilted her head, giving him a sideways look before stalking through the newly cleared rows of graves. She stopped and checked behind her. "Are you coming?"

"Yes ma'am, Miss Peggy." He ran to catch up.

They strolled through the rows, Peggy explaining tombstone inscriptions and telling stories about all the dearly departed, especially her relatives. She was careful not to recall all the infant graves in her various ancestral plots, but she noticed Joseph surreptitiously studying the dates on each marker.

At the end opposite the church, they reached the rows that Peggy had not yet cleared. "You know, I can help you finish if you'd like the help," Joseph said. "And the company."

"I would like that, Joseph. But while I've been doing this, it's felt almost like I'm on a mission. Like there's something here I'm supposed to find."

"Like what?"

"I don't know. All I know is that I haven't found it yet."

"Maybe with the two of us looking, we can find it faster."

"I appreciate that, but I think this is a job I need to finish myself."

Joseph shrugged. "The offer stands." He walked Peggy to the manse door.

"Would you like to come in for a while? We could watch some television."

Joseph stroked her hair and brushed his lips across her forehead. "I'd love nothing more. But I don't want anybody talking about you more than they already are. Besides, I don't know if I trust myself to watch televison." He winked. "I'd be too busy watching you."

Peggy was wrestling a stubborn bramble when two trucks pulled up in front of the cemetery, one specially constructed to transport the windows, each swathed in thick white padding. A crew of men spilled from the second truck. As she slapped the dirt from her palms, Joseph and Otha Lee met the workers, who shook hands heartily with Joseph but ignored Otha Lee, who held his hand out to an aloof response.

Peggy started toward the truck when she was seized with an unwelcome anxiety. Her spine stiffened and her chest felt weak. She ran into the house and leaned against the kitchen sink, gulping air, trying to get her heart to slow down. A knock at the back door further startled her. Turning, she saw Joseph staring at her through the screen.

"The windows are here. Don't you want to come look?" He came in and placed his rough hands on her shoulders. "Why are you shaking? Ain't nothing to be scared of. They're your windows."

"Oh really. I had forgotten." She laughed nervously, turning to wash her hands vigorously. "Suddenly it's like I can't look. A drawing is one thing, but a physical manifestation of something is another."

Joseph hugged her and kissed the top of her head, her hands leaving wet prints on his shirt. "Peggy, I know they're going to be beautiful. Anything coming from your heart has to be beautiful. You trust me, don't you?"

"Yes, I trust you. It's me I don't trust."

"We'll just have to work with that." He walked to the door. "You coming?"

Peggy took a deep breath and gulped a glass of water. "Right now."

The workmen unloaded the first window and carefully removed the wrappings, holding it both steadily and gingerly at the same time. Otha Lee, Peggy, and Joseph watched as the details slowly emerged. The head of the biblical Joseph. The Virgin Mary. The baby Jesus. Their small donkey on the dusty flight into Egypt. Otha Lee gazed in wonder, waiting until they completely removed the wrapping and had propped the window carefully against the church's outer wall.

"Oh, Miss Peggy," he whispered, his eyes flowing over the sparkling glass, reaching toward it with a trembling hand, stopping just short of touching. "Such a wondrous sight. I don't know when I've seen such a thing."

"Is it okay, Otha Lee? Do you really like it?"

"Are they all the same?"

"No, each is different. I tried to portray all the great Bible stories."

"Miss Peggy, if they're all as spectacular as this one, ain't gonna be no need for my preaching, 'cause the congregation can just stare in awe and wonder at these here windows." He slowly backed away. Joseph squeezed Peggy's arm, then left to help remove the old windows. The job boss walked by, then came back.

"Are you Peggy Nickles?"

"I am."

"We need you to tell us which windows you want where." He handed her a clipboard. "If you'll sketch out a floor plan with some arrows, then we won't have to keep bothering you."

Peggy smiled and handed back the clipboard. "This is Mr. Otha Lee Sturgis. Reverend Sturgis, that is. He'll be making those decisions."

Otha Lee's eyes widened. "Miss Peggy, I think it'd be better if you do the deciding."

"Yes, ma'am, Miss Peggy," the foreman said, smirking. "I'd rather take orders from a bossy white lady than a nigger any day of the week."

"Sir, I will thank you not to speak that way while you are on this job."

"Is there a problem?" Joseph came and stood between Otha Lee and the foreman.

"No," Otha Lee said quickly. "Miss Peggy, I think it would be better if I went on home. Y'all don't need me here today anyway." He turned and walked toward his truck, Peggy following.

"Otha Lee, don't let that ignorant trash run you off. You know you might face a lot worse."

"I know, Miss Peggy. Believe you me, I have. But you know that expression about the devil you know and the devil you don't?"

"I believe so."

"I don't know him. I know what ones to look for 'round here." He climbed in the truck and rumbled off.

"What's that old nigger preacher to this church?" the foreman said to Joseph, glancing to see if anyone else was listening. "What's he to that Peggy woman?"

Joseph thrust a finger into the man's chest. "Peggy designed those windows. Otha Lee ain't none of your concern, and I'll thank you not to use that word again while you're here." Joseph caught himself from telling the plans for the church, fearing retaliation from the crew who had come to put the very expensive crowning touch on the old sanctuary.

Peggy came back and snatched the clipboard away from the foreman. Sitting on the stump, she hurriedly sketched out the window placement. She explained it to Joseph before handing it back to the foreman. "Make sure he doesn't botch it up," she said quietly before returning to the cemetery, where she violently chopped vines for the rest of the morning.

Otha Lee walked in the house to find Otis still sprawled across his bed, fast asleep. Since the revival meeting, Otis had said few words, and the words he did say weren't what Otha Lee wanted to hear. He had hoped that by telling the truth about his own past and his reason for accepting the gift of the church, he might motivate Otis to opening his heart toward the Lord and softening his attitude toward Miss Peggy. He feared that he had only succeeded in antagonizing his son, driving him toward a more militant position. At one point, Otis had even called him an Uncle Tom. He refused to let Otis see how much the remark stung and chose instead to forgive his son, chalking his position up to his raising, one uninformed by the realities of growing up in Bonham.

Moving quietly, he edged up to Otis's desk and picked up a sheaf of papers laying next to the typewriter. He read for several minutes, mouthing words to himself until Otis stirred and realized he was not alone.

"You're not supposed to be reading that, Pops," he said, rubbing his eyes before letting out a huge yawn.

"Why not? Ain't it going to be published anyway? Might as well read it now as well as then."

"That's beside the point. It is a work in progress, and I do not like anybody reading my work until it is finished." He sat on the edge of the bed and stared at Otha Lee who was now seated in the desk chair. "But since you already peeked, you might as well go on and tell me what you think."

"Your typing's terrible. 'Bout every other word is misspelled."

Otis nodded in agreement. "I'm planning to get a professional secretary to fix it."

"That would be advisable." He tossed the papers back on the pile.

"What about the content?"

"All I can say is you got nerve."

"Nerve?"

"Live up north your whole life, then think you can come back down here for two months and get a sense of two hundred years of hard-wrought history?"

"So I take it you don't agree with my interpretation of life in Bonham, South Carolina."

"Son, it's going to take a lot longer than two months for you to get the real feel of anything around here."

Otis sat silently, watching a bluebird through the front window, flying from ground to tree limb and back.

"Son, you got something on your mind?"

Otis shrugged and laughed softly. "I hope I'm not wearing out my welcome. I know I haven't been much help to you."

"Where did this come from all of a sudden?"

Otis took a deep breath, then spoke slowly. "There's something I ought to tell you. I should have told you when I arrived."

"Ain't never too late to be telling the truth."

"I got a wife back in Detroit."

"A wife?"

"Yes, a wife, and a daughter. Thirteen years old."

"A daughter? You mean I got a grandbaby and you didn't bring her here to see her old washed-up grandpa?"

"It's a little more complicated than that."

Otha Lee squinted. "Just how complicated?"

"Her mother and I—we're separated. Truth is, she threw me out."

Otha Lee considered the remark. It hung there like an icicle melting on a spring morning.

"What did you do to cause her to throw you out?"

Otis drew back. "What makes you think I did something?"

"'Cause a woman don't ordinarily throw a man out on the street unless he's done something really stupid or extremely grievous. Or both. Now which is it?"

"Stupid or grievous?"

"Yep."

"Both."

"It's another woman, ain't it?"

"How'd you guess?"

"That's about the most stupid, grievous thing a man can do to a woman who has stood beside him all their married life and bore him a child." He stood and turned as if to walk out.

"You might want to sit back down."

Otha Lee looked up. "You mean there's more?" He prayed silently. "Lord, I done got me a job now." He looked back at Otis, who was staring down at his hands as if in prayer, too.

"The other girl—she's pregnant."

Otha Lee nodded.

"I lost my job."

Otha Lee nodded again. "So in other words, the main reason you came home wasn't to write a book, it was to run away from your real home and your real mess and your real life."

Otis lay back down. Otha Lee regarded him for several seconds. Then leaning over, he grabbed the footboard solidly by the bottom rung.

"What are you doing down there, Pops?" Otis reared up on his elbows.

Otha Lee did not reply. Saying a silent prayer, he lifted the bed and with a shout pushed it over, causing Otis to land in a cowering heap under the window.

"Pops, what's wrong with you?" He rubbed his elbows and knees.

"Ain't nothing wrong with me, boy. It's what's wrong with you." He grabbed Otis by his arms and dragged him across the room, throwing him into the chair. He leaned down and fixed his eyes on Otis, who tried looking away but failed in the face of his determined father.

"You lied to me."

"I know, Pops, but—"

"Be quiet and listen, and you hear what I am saying to you." His fingers dug into Otis's shoulders. "You lied to me. You lied to your wife. You lied to your daughter. You lied to yourself. You committed adultery. You did not honor your father or the memory of your mother." He let go of Otis. "Boy, you're in even worse shape than I thought you was."

"It's got nothing to do with you, Pops."

"How can you sit there and say it ain't got nothing to do with me when you done come down here and hid out in my house, pretending like your life is all hunky-dory when you done made a mess of everything? And ain't even told me so I don't even know to help you." He sighed. "I knew you needed help. I just didn't know you needed this much help."

"I'm sorry, Pops." Otis sounded like a schoolboy caught smoking in the rest room.

"Yeah, I'm sorry, too." Otha Lee rubbed his hand up and down his face. "If I'd've known all this, I wouldn't have spent the summer rebuilding a church. I would have spent it rebuilding you."

"Ain't that what you been trying to do? Dragging me to church every time I turn around. Aiming sermons at me."

"Yeah, I admit I been trying to put the fear of the Lord back into you. And not having much success, either."

Otis stood and retrieved his clothes from the nail driven into the back of the door. Otha Lee sat back down at the desk. "So what you planning to do about it?"

"About what? My book? Finish it, I guess."

"I ain't talking 'bout no book. That's your problem, son; you looking to words for answers instead of doing something to set your life straight."

Otis shook out his shirt and pulled it on, lining up the buttons carefully from the bottom. "I thought maybe if I came back here, the place that's supposed to be my home, I might figure out what to do."

"So you come to any conclusions?"

He sat on the bed and put his head in his hands. "No conclusions. Just more questions. And it seems like there are no answers."

Otha Lee placed a gnarled hand on Otis's shoulder. "Maybe you just ain't looked to the right source yet."

seventeen

The first fallen leaves of autumn created a thin amber carpet that covered the newly cleared cemetery grounds. It had taken a lot of work, and Peggy's back had paid dearly, but she was approaching the end of her task.

Across the way, the work crew continued installing the windows, each more spectacular than the last. Now and then Joseph would catch her eye and nod approvingly. Peggy was afraid to examine the windows up close for fear she had committed some major theological folly that was now manifested in glass for the world and Otha Lee's congregation to view forever.

Instead she bent intensely to the graveyard cleanup. As her work progressed, she became more maudlin at the discovery of so many infant graves. So many from her own family. She marveled that she and her sisters had survived, as had Gail, and indeed that enough Nickles had lived to continue the family bloodline.

Peggy had often heard of maladies that ran in families, illnesses that caused all the babies to perish within a few days of birth, or for an entire generation of children to be struck by some terrible cancer during the teenage years. At times, she felt that her family had been cursed, that perhaps they were paying for the sins of ancient fathers with the lives of their daughters and sons.

She hacked at the weeds in the last row. They had dried out, not just from the drought but from the gradual change in seasons, and were easy to pull up. Peggy raked them into a pile she planned to burn before the

November rains began. She scarcely paused to look up at the names, deciding she would return later and transcribe the inscriptions for posterity, as many had begun to fade and wear away under the pressures of time and weather. More than once, she had asked Joseph and Otha Lee to right a stone that had fallen, as if it had grown weary of its task and tumbled down, asking to be laid to rest itself.

Halfway through the row, Peggy stopped and sat on the ground to rest in the shade of a sycamore. Wiping her forehead, she looked up briefly, then again slowly, her eyes drawn to the monument before her.

Douglas Dean Hayworth
1916–1942
Died in the Service of His Country
World War 2

She crawled to the stone on her hands and knees, and rubbed her hands across the inscription. "Doug," she whispered, as a tear trickled off her chin, making raindrop spots on her pale blue blouse.

After a while, Peggy sat back and pulled her knees against her chest, rocking back and forth, back and forth, as her mind and memories ebbed to a day twelve years earlier when it seemed life had just begun and her heart was so full of love, she didn't think anything could take it away.

It was a sunny November day, one of those days when the sky is such a brilliant shade of blue that it is easy to believe the universe is endless. Peggy stood in the backyard, hanging wet diapers on the clothesline as Becky lay cooing on a blanket under the maple tree ablaze with crimson foliage. Doug had joined in the mad enlistment rush after December 7, 1941, enraged by the bombing at Pearl Harbor like everyone else, leaving her pregnant and alone with a promise that after he saved the world from evil tyrants and made it a safe place for their firstborn, they would spend the rest of their lives together making love and making babies until their home burst with laughter and family.

Peggy had believed him. She felt in her heart that he would come back to her and be there for her, as he had been since they were children, when she first knew she loved him. Raised next door to each other, they had grown up in the moneyed part of town but vowed that money would not be the center of their life together as it had been for their parents and friends.

When she finished hanging out the wash, she had lain down with Becky and looked through the tree at the deep blue sky. She talked to Becky about Daddy, as she often did, as if by the simple act of speaking to her baby she could create a memory of the man her child had never seen. Becky soon drifted to sleep, and a chill invaded the Indian summer day. She lifted the baby gently and turned to go inside, only to find herself facing a Navy chaplain and another man in uniform whose name and rank failed to register. The days after that became a blank.

When she came to, regaining a consciousness of her own existence, Peggy was in a hospital bed, a doctor observing her through thick-lensed eyeglasses.

"Where's my baby?" she whispered, her voice distant, as if it belonged to someone else.

Dr. Spencer leaned over and asked how she was feeling. Peggy replied that she couldn't remember coming to this place. She looked out the window, astonished to see crepe myrtles covered with hot pink blooms. She walked over to it unsteadily and placed the tips of her fingers against the glass.

"Your family will be glad to know that your condition has improved." The doctor stood beside her, his head slightly raised now, as if examining her through the semicircles of his bifocals. Peggy felt dizzy and sat back down on the bed.

"What happened to me? Why is it summer instead of winter?"

"You had what's called in laymen's terms a nervous breakdown. The news of your husband's death created such a trauma that your mind could not handle it. You have been heavily sedated for much of your time here."

"Where is here?" She laid down and pulled the sheet up to her chin.

"Clairmont Oaks. A private psychiatric hospital."

Peggy nodded, sipping water to ease the cottonball feeling in her mouth. She felt displaced in time, unsure of what she had done, or had had done to her, in the intervening months.

"You didn't answer my question."

"I think we have talked enough now. We have begun cutting back the sedatives. It will take a while for your mind and body to readjust." He nodded to a nurse Peggy had not noticed before, who approached with a syringe and quickly stabbed it in Peggy's arm.

Over the next several days, Peggy felt more lucid, still wondering where Becky was but realizing it would be of no use to push the doctor, who seemed reluctant to fill her in on any missing details of the "lost months," as she came to call them.

After a few days, they went outside, as the air cooled into September, and she realized she was somewhere far up in the mountains, away from home, away from where her parents and sisters could easily visit. She asked Dr. Spencer when she could return home.

"It will be a while yet, Peggy." He stared into the distance. "We still have much to deal with here."

Between sessions, Peggy thought hard, trying to remember whatever it was she needed to remember so that the doctor might be spared the trouble of telling her. One Saturday afternoon, the nurse came into her room and announced that she had visitors.

Peggy looked in the mirror, appalled at her appearance, how gaunt and pale and thrown away she looked. She straightened herself out as best she could and went into the common area where she found Belva and Beatrice waiting side by side, clutching their identical patent leather purses.

"Oh, Peggy," they whispered in unison, hugging her so that she felt a poplin-clad two-headed creature had embraced her instead of her overwrought identical twin sisters. Peggy smiled and led them outside, where the air was not medicinal and her sisters wouldn't be intimidated by some of the other patients, who could be quite intrusive, depending upon whatever delusion they were suffering from that day.

Beatrice smiled nervously. "We would have come sooner, but gas is rationed. For the war effort, you know."

"How are you, Peggy?" Belva said, placing a white-gloved palm on her forearm. Beatrice did the same on her left side.

"I'd be better if I could remember whatever it is I've forgotten."

The twins fell silent at this response, glancing from each other to Peggy.

"How are Mother and Daddy?"

"They're doing fairly well," Belva said.

"They miss you terribly," added Beatrice. "They wanted to come, but Daddy's having a time with his back. He didn't think he could stand the trip."

"No, of course not. And Eva?"

"Eva's Eva," Belva said.

"Some days more so than others," said Beatrice, and they all broke into nervous laughter.

Peggy stopped and looked first at one twin, then the other. "Dr. Spencer won't tell me anything at all about Becky. How is my baby? I know one of you must be taking care of her." She walked to a nearby table, sat down, and wrung her hands. "I miss her. She must have forgotten me by now."

Belva and Beatrice sat silently. A river of starlings flying south darkened the eastern sky. They watched as the birds undulated, swooping and sweeping their way toward sun and warmth.

"I want to go home with you," Peggy said, getting up and heading toward the parking lot. "We can leave now, and I can see Becky today."

Beatrice motioned for Belva to fetch the doctor as she pursued Peggy across the leaf-strewn lawn. "Where's your car?" Peggy demanded as she scurried from vehicle to vehicle, looking for Bea's familiar black Buick. Finally she spotted it and climbed into the backseat, waiting expectantly for her sisters to take her home.

Dr. Spencer opened the passenger door and stuck in his head. "Mind if I sit with you, Peggy?"

"Are you planning to go back to Bonham with us? Daddy must be paying you quite well."

Dr. Spencer laughed softly and sat beside her.

"Why won't anyone tell me how Becky is or where she is?"

"We were trying to wait until you were more stable."

"I'm stable. Now you tell me about my baby so I can quit imagining what is going on or I'm going to get unstable again real quick."

The psychiatrist opened the door again and slid out, letting in a cold burst of wind. "Let's go inside and talk." The twins stood behind him, hands clenched together and together. Peggy slowly got out and stared at them, her anxious sisters, and the always even Dr. Spencer.

"She's dead, isn't she?" Peggy watched their faces. No one spoke. "She died because I wasn't there to love her." She walked away from the group, back toward the courtyard, then stopped. "Did you bury her next to Doug?" she asked, not looking back.

"She's close to her father," Belva said, her voice breaking.

"Good." Then Peggy went back inside, to her room, where she stayed for another year, until her grief became a burden, and her will to live finally outstripped the heaviness of her soul.

"Peggy?"

Joseph knelt next to her, running his rough hand up and down her arm. Peggy sat still, crying silent tears as the tombstone came slowly back into focus. Joseph looked over and read the epitaph. "He must have been someone special to you."

Peggy nodded, wiping her face with the edge of her sleeve. "He was my husband. He died in the war."

"I'm sorry. I didn't know."

"I'm surprised Otha Lee didn't tell you."

Joseph shrugged. "I guess he figured you'd tell me in your own time."

Peggy scrambled to her knees, looking to each side of the grave. Joseph followed her eyes, wondering what she was looking for.

"I don't see it," Peggy said, now standing, roaming back and forth along the row, peering through what was left of the thick weeds and undergrowth.

"See what?" Joseph said, following her. "Tell me what you're trying to find, and I'll help you look."

"Becky's grave." She walked back to the Hayworth plot. "It has to be here. They told me she was close to him."

"Peggy." Joseph stood beside her, grabbed her by a shoulder and turned her to face him. "Tell me what's going on so I can help you. Now who is Becky?"

"Our daughter. Mine and Doug's. Becky—Rebecca Hayworth. Now help me find it."

"You're telling me your daughter died and you don't know where the grave is? Didn't you go to the funeral?"

Peggy began to shake. "I didn't go to either of their funerals. I was—away."

"Away?"

"The Clairmont Oaks Hospital for the Mentally Insane." She pressed her hands across her mouth. "In all these years, I have never told that to anyone." She laughed ruefully. "Although I'm fairly sure everyone in Bonham probably knows anyway."

"Why would you be put away?" He guided her to the stumps where they sat facing each other.

"When the military came to tell me Doug had been killed in action—I just collapsed inside myself. Becky was a baby. I couldn't move I was in such shock. Doug and I grew up together. I had known him practically from the time we could walk." Her voice fell to a whisper. "I had never loved anyone else. It was like a big piece of me had been shot away."

Joseph took her hand. "Go on."

"Like I said, I couldn't move. They have a fancy name for it— catatonia. I couldn't care for Becky. My little girl." She stared into the middle distance, focusing on the past. "My family took her. But when they put me away, when I came out of it, I found out she had died, too. So I had nothing left."

"How long were you in the hospital?"

"Two years."

Joseph let out a low whistle.

Peggy started back toward the graveyard. "The thing is, I thought my family would have buried her near Doug. She's not here."

"Is it possible the grave could be unmarked?"

"No, not in my family. All the most dominating tombstones belong to my family."

Joseph stood behind her, his hands on her shoulders. "Why don't you ask your sisters? They would know, wouldn't they?"

Peggy nodded, her shoulders shaking as the tears flowed. "I did, but they wouldn't tell me." She thought back to her meeting with Milo Percy and wondered how much he knew.

"Do you want me to go with you?"

Peggy wiped her eyes. "No." She turned and gave Joseph a strained smile. "I'm sorry I didn't tell you all this before."

Joseph looked away. "We all have our secrets, Peggy." He hugged her, kissing her lightly on the mouth, and watched as she walked, first hesitantly, then purposefully toward her car and drove away. He turned back to the church, the windows now in place. He went inside, wondering whether to be dazzled or humbled by the artistic windows. The foreman came inside as well.

"You best be closing those storm shutters," he said, strolling past the windows, examining each for flaws or cracks.

"Why's that? This is the prettiest day I seen in months."

"That's deceiving. Ain't you heard?"

"Heard what?"

"There's a hurricane coming. Hazel. Supposed to be hitting about tonight." He motioned to Joseph to follow him outside. "Look at that sky."

Joseph studied the low-lying clouds.

"Tropical clouds," the foreman explained. "Wind's already picking up. Means we'll be packing up." The crew had already gathered their tools.

"I ain't ever been through a hurricane," Joseph said. "I hope it don't blow the church down."

"I doubt it'll blow that church down," the foreman said. "I would be more worried about all those trees 'round your galfriend's house yonder." He winked. "Might be safer if y'all spent the night in the church tonight." He walked off hurriedly before Joseph could react to the tone of the last remark.

eighteen

Peggy paced the length of Beatrice's parlor. The twins perched on the edge of the settee like two identical parakeets awaiting judgment after committing mischief while their owner was away.

"So answer me," Peggy said, stopping in front of them. "Where did you all bury my baby?"

Belva cleared her throat. "You'll need to ask Eva."

"What's Eva got to do with it?"

"Mother and Daddy weren't well then, either, you know," said Beatrice, wringing a handkerchief.

Belva said, "So Mr. Percy was your legal guardian while you were hospitalized."

"Mr. Percy instead of Mother and Daddy. Why didn't they appoint one of you as my guardian?" Peggy resumed pacing.

"They thought he might be better at handling your—situation," Belva replied.

"Like what? Making sure I stayed put away so I couldn't ever find out the truth about my daughter?"

"You couldn't handle it then," Belva said.

Peggy threw up her hands. "I can handle it now. So why don't you stop stalling and tell me where my daughter is buried?"

Belva and Beatrice looked at each other before Beatrice said, "We just think you should talk to Eva about it."

"Now I'm convinced something's up," Peggy said, placing her hands on her hips. "You can't tell me something simple like where Becky is buried?"

Belva began to quiver and scooted closer to her twin, who placed an arm around her shoulders.

"Tell me," Peggy said quietly, kneeling and placing her hands on her sisters' knees. "Just tell me."

"She's not buried," Belva whispered.

"She's not what?" Peggy said, straining to hear.

"She's not dead," Beatrice said, her eyes brimming with tears.

Peggy rocked back on her heels. "If this is a joke, it's not funny."

"She didn't die," Beatrice said again, breaking into sobs.

"If she didn't die, then what happened to her?"

"Talk to Eva," Belva said, rising and walking from the room.

Beatrice took Peggy's hand. "I want you to know, Peggy, we didn't—we don't—approve of what she did."

Peggy snatched her hand away. "I can see if I want any answers about Becky, I'll *have* to ask Eva. As if she'll be any more honest than the two of you."

Eva was sitting behind the broad mahogany desk in her study, going through the household accounts, when Peggy walked in, quickly outpacing the maid. Eva waved her away.

Peggy planted her palms on the desk's slick surface. "You tell me now what happened to Becky."

"My word," Eva said, taking off her glasses and folding them slowly. "After all these years, you finally mention her name."

"I thought she was dead."

"Thought?"

"Yes. Until today when I was cleaning the last of the graves and found Doug's but not Becky's. Then our sisters inform me that there is no grave because my child is not dead. They insist you are the one with all the answers." She barked out a laugh. "Not that that's anything unusual. At least from your point of view."

Eva nodded. "So what is it you wish to know?"

Peggy's eyes flashed. "For the last twelve years, all of you led me to believe that my daughter was dead, and today I find out she's alive." She leaned over Eva's chair. "Did you give her away? Is there no chance I will ever see her again?" Her voice rose. "Where is Becky?"

Eva folded her hands in her lap. "You were ill. You couldn't care for yourself, much less your child."

"Where is she?"

"She's at boarding school."

Peggy straightened. "Boarding school? You mean with Gail?"

"Your daughter didn't die." Eva rubbed her eyes and sighed. "Mine did."

A silence fell between them. The wind rose and cracked against the windowpanes. Peggy heard a door slam somewhere in the house, as if suddenly all the air had been sucked out.

"Are you telling me that Gail is Becky?"

"She's not Becky anymore. She hasn't been Becky since the day you went crazy and Mother and Daddy had to put you away."

Peggy sat heavily. "Gail—your Gail—died. While I was in the hospital."

Eva nodded, her face suddenly weary.

"You took my daughter and gave her your daughter's name and raised her as your own." Peggy's eyes scanned the floor. "I don't remember giving anyone permission to give away my daughter."

"Milo Percy."

"Mr. Percy. How could he . . ."

"He was your legal guardian."

"He was authorized to take away my child? Where were Mother and Daddy in all this?"

"They decided. We all thought it was best."

"Best for whom? For my child never to know her mother? For my daughter to believe she's the daughter of a witch like you? For my child to be sent away like she's not even wanted at home? That she isn't worthy enough to be raised among her own family and friends?"

"If you're waiting for me to apologize, it's not going to happen."

"I'm getting her back."

"You can't. The adoption's permanent and binding."

"And probably illegal. Eva, dear sister, nothing is permanent." Peggy laughed quietly. "Not even death, although you took a shot at that."

Eva came around the desk, pointing a finger in Peggy's face. "Gail is my child. *My* child. I raised her and fed her and clothed her and disciplined her for nearly her entire life."

"You left an important word out of that list—*love*. You never once said that you loved her. Not to me. Not even to her."

"Love comes through action, not words. I am the only mother she has ever known or will ever know."

Peggy slapped Eva's hand away. "That will change. It will. I gave birth to her, and I have always loved her as if she were my own. One day she even told me she wished I were her mother." She backed away as heavy raindrops splattered against the window glass. "If only I had known I was." She spun around and ran out, Eva running after, the wind pulling the screen door away and slamming it against the wall.

"You will not destroy her life, Peggy. I will not allow it!"

Peggy yanked open the car door and leaned over the roof. "I won't be destroying her life. You already did that with your lies. I'll just be giving it back."

Otha Lee's anxiety was rising with the howling winds. Otis had taken off earlier in the day, leaving Otha Lee without transportation and worried about his son's state of mind. He knelt in the middle of the floor.

"Dear Lord, dearest heavenly Father. I didn't raise my son, didn't guide him to the right and righteous path. He has done wrong, but so have I, Lord help me, so have I. I tried not to judge when he told me, but I did, and now he's out there in the storm. Help him find his way back, Lord, to me and to you. In Jesus' name, Amen."

Otha Lee pulled himself back to his feet. For a moment, the wind calmed, and he thought he heard the truck coming down the road. He ran onto the porch, only to see Joseph driving up on his motorcycle, soaked to the skin. The machine skidded to a halt, and Joseph sprinted up the steps.

"Oooeeee!" he shouted. "One heckuva blow coming on, Otha Lee." Joseph noted Otha Lee looking toward the turnoff. "What're you looking for?"

"Otis. He done run off in my truck, and I don't know if he's coming back."

"We best leave him a note, then."

"A note? Where we going?"

"To the church. I hate to say it, but I don't think this old house is going to stand up to a hurricane, even with the repairs we made."

Otha Lee nodded, absently scanning the tar-papered shack.

"You got a raincoat? I was hoping we could go back in your truck, but I reckon my cycle'll have to do."

"Let me go see to my hogs and we'll go." Just then a heavy outburst obliterated the road. "Maybe we better wait a few minutes. I think we got time before it gets real bad. Come on inside."

Joseph started to sit, then remembered his sopping clothes. Otha Lee sat uneasily, listening to the wind whistling in the eaves.

"Can I ask you something about Peggy, Otha Lee?"

"Don't know that I can answer, but I'll try."

"Did you know she was married once?"

Otha Lee sat back and rocked. "Thought everybody knew that. Douglas Hayworth. Only family in town—maybe the county—had more money than the Nickles. They had a child, too. Name of Becky."

"Peggy said she died. While she was away."

"In the hospital, you mean."

Joseph nodded.

"The baby didn't die."

Joseph stepped forward, leaving a puddle in his wake. "Are you saying Peggy's lying?"

"I ain't said she's lying. That's just what all that money-hungry family of hers has led her to believe."

"Still, how could her daughter be alive and her not know it?"

"A family like the Nickles specializes in secrets. What other people don't know won't hurt them." Otha Lee chuckled. "Only thing is, they don't know how word gets around. Everybody knew the child ain't dead but poor old Miss Peggy."

"But how . . ."

"Miss Eva and Miss Peggy had baby girls at the same time. Mr. Doug, he got killed in the war, and Miss Peggy done went and lost her mind. Her mama and papa stuck her away in one of them insane hospitals.

"Before long, Miss Eva's girl, Gail, ups and dies. You seen all them baby graves in the burying ground? There's some kind of curse in that family. Babies been dying for no reason for years and years. My grandmama, she a slave owned by the Nickles when the Civil War came and she tell me about dressing out babies for the grave."

They listened as the deluge began to pass. Otha Lee continued.

"Miss Eva, she full of grief and caring for Becky anyway. The twins were too childlike themselves to care for babies. They each lost one already and was too afraid of the family curse to risk having more. So Miss Eva convinces everybody to go along with her in getting Becky adopted as her own. Tries to convince everybody it's in Peggy's best interest for the child to 'die,' seeing as how she ain't got no husband anymore."

"Peggy found her husband's grave in the cemetery this morning. I found her scrambling around, saying she couldn't find her daughter's. She went to see her sisters about it." Joseph ran his hands through his drenched hair. "Let me ask you this. If you knew about her daughter, then why didn't you tell Peggy? I mean, she really trusts you."

Otha Lee sighed and pulled a raincoat from the peg in the kitchen. "Wasn't my place to tell her. I thought about it, but family secrets are best told by the family that started 'em." He stood at the screen door. "We best be getting on to the church then. She done found out the truth by now." He shook his head. " 'Ye shall know the truth and the truth shall make you free,' says the good book."

Joseph opened the door carefully and peered into the blowing rain. "Too bad it had to come at the price of so many lies."

nineteen

Peggy sat on the front pew, staring up at the new pulpit. The wind pounded against the closed shutters, rattling the hinges, but Peggy's mind was elsewhere, in Virginia, with her daughter.

Gail. *Her* daughter. She couldn't imagine how her own sister could have done such a thing. It had been bad enough that her parents had taken away her art, and the war her husband, but to take a baby away from her mother to replace another—Peggy couldn't comprehend it.

She knew what she would do. She would get another lawyer. Milo Percy, with his smiling lies. Peggy wondered whom she could trust now. Otha Lee, Joseph—at least they hadn't lied. She didn't think so.

The lost years. She had spent plenty of time with Becky—Gail—so much time. Why couldn't she have seen it herself? In the eyes, the mannerisms. Surely Gail bore a resemblance to her or Doug, or both.

Leaning forward, Peggy cradled her head in her hands. "Oh, dear Lord," she cried. "Why did this happen to me? Why did you let this happen to me?"

After a while, she raised her head and realized how dark the church had become. Searching a box they had taken from the old altar furnishings, she found two tarnished candlesticks, dusty candles, and matches. She lit the candles and walked slowly up and down the aisle, holding the light up to see the stained glass windows. They appeared flat and dull, lifeless, not the inspiration to worship she had hoped.

The letter. She reached into her pocket and pulled out the letter that had arrived that morning from Gail, who was at boarding school. Holding it near the light, she read it, thinking of the verse from 1 Corinthians 13: "For now we see through a glass, darkly; but then face to face." Perhaps she had been too close to see it, to see her own daughter. Too close to see the truth.

"I hope that when I come back to Bonham, you and I can spend more time together," Gail had written. "It's almost like we're sisters, Aunt Peggy. I feel like you and I are a part of each other. Like you fill in some of my missing pieces."

Sisters. It had seemed that way. But it was more, so much more. The bond of mother and child had been broken, and Peggy knew that while it would take some legal maneuvering to straighten out the mess Eva had made, the spiritual bond was already in place.

She was startled from her musings when the old oak doors creaked at the rear of the sanctuary. It took both Otha Lee and Joseph's strength to open them against the gale-force winds.

"Thank God," Joseph said, spotting Peggy. "We went to the house to get you and saw your car. Figured you must have come on over here."

"It must be getting worse outside," Peggy said absently, placing the candles on the communion table.

"Miss Peggy, it's a gully-washer out yonder. Joseph didn't think my house was safe, nor yours either, so we're holding out hope the Lord's house is going to bring us through."

They stood in the vestibule, dripping water onto an old tarpaulin. Joseph pulled some cellophane-wrapped packs of cookies and crackers from his pocket and tossed them onto a pew. "That's supper, y'all. Don't eat it all at once. We don't know how long we're going to be holed up here. Might have to be breakfast, too."

"Miss Peggy, you looking a mite pale," said Otha Lee.

She put her palms to her cheeks. "It's a wonder I'm not fallen dead."

"Did you talk to your sisters?" Joseph asked cautiously.

Peggy nodded. "I learned quite a bit more than I care to know."

Otha Lee sat on a pew. "Miss Eva finally told you about Gail."

Peggy sucked in her breath. "You mean you knew?" She sighed. "I guess Daddy told you."

"Lots of folks knew," Otha Lee said, nodding and rubbing his chin. "Just ain't nobody asked. And it wasn't our place to tell."

"It's hard to find out the truth when you're asking the wrong questions," added Joseph.

"My problem was that I didn't ask sooner," Peggy said, tears rolling off her chin.

Joseph put his arm around her until she pulled away, wiping her eyes. "Where's Otis, Otha Lee?"

"I don't rightly know."

"He took off in Otha Lee's truck, and we had to ride my motorcycle up here."

"No wonder you're so sopping. If I'd had more presence of mind, I'd have come and gotten you myself."

"Some things are more important, Miss Peggy."

The storm strengthened then, the sound of the wind dimming their voices, pressing the church on all sides. Peggy felt as if the hurricane were squeezing her between two giant hands. Shuttered, the church's gloom continued to intensify as night set in, and the storm swallowed the night in a darkness of its own.

Joseph sat to himself, grappling for words to ease Peggy's pain. Otha Lee had also grown silent as they listened to the sharp wind and driving rain argue their successive points. Yet the church felt solid, safe, the haven each of them needed.

"Peggy," Joseph said quietly, "Otha Lee." The others sat on the front pews, on opposite sides of the aisle.

"Yes, son?" Otha Lee said, as if he had been expecting something all along.

"I know this probably ain't the right time to tell y'all this, but I been waiting for months, and I don't know that there'll ever be a right time."

"Joseph, I don't believe there's anything else that could shock me after the day I've just had." Peggy sounded drained, her voice distant although she sat only a few yards away.

Joseph took a deep breath and said a silent prayer. "When I told you I'd been living in Columbia, I never did tell you where."

"I just assumed it was some boardinghouse or something," said Otha Lee.

"I wish it had been." He sat silently for a moment as they listened to the wind's rising and falling howl. "I was in prison."

"How could you have been in prison, Joseph?" Peggy turned and looked into his eyes. "I can't imagine you doing anything that would land you there."

"I don't think it's so much what I did but what I tried to do that made it all look like it did."

Peggy shook her head.

"I done lost track of where this is going." Otha Lee came around to sit next to Joseph.

"Then I guess I better go back to the beginning," Joseph said, as the memory of the day that changed his life floated to the surface and broke through, only to be quieted by the tempest that brewed overhead.

"I had a younger brother. His name was Brett," he began, the gusting winds outside recalling that day in March. "I was late getting home from school one day. Brett had gone home early, claiming he was sick. He used to do that a lot. I was late because I had stayed after class to help my shop teacher—his name was Mr. Knott—I was helping him make a cabinet for one of his other classes."

"He must have taught you well," Peggy said, taking his calloused hand between hers. "Of course, the evidence is all around us."

"He was the best thing in my life then." He ran his hands through his hair. "I would have been the first in my family to finish high school." He went silent for a moment before continuing. "When I got home, Brett wasn't nowhere around, as usual. He never did chores. I always wound up doing his and mine both.

I went in the kitchen and started eating a cold biscuit." He shrugged. "I don't even know why I remember that. I guess it's because when Mama asked me where Brett was, I told her I reckoned he was off being his usual lazy self somewhere. Mama came over and slapped that biscuit plumb out of my hand.

"She always did favor Brett. She was always claiming he was feeling poorly and he didn't have to do chores if he didn't feel like it." He paused and looked up at Peggy, trying to gauge her reaction. She was watching him with concern, as was Otha Lee. "Anyway, she told me to go out and shoot a rabbit for supper. We had an old fishing shack down on the river, and she told me to go and see if Brett was there. So I got the rifle and went out hunting.

"It was warm and calm, prettiest March day you ever saw," he said, stopping to listen to the wind howl. "I found a rabbit pretty quick in a little clearing. I shot it and then went on down to the shack. Brett was sitting on the dock." Joseph rubbed his hands over his face. "He started cussing me on account of he thought I was sweet on some girl that he liked. She was sweet on me, but I didn't care much for her, and I told him he could have her.

"He started crying. He was always crying, over the least little things." He took a deep breath. "I never understood that. Why some people are always sad or scared, when there ain't nothing to be sad or scared about.

"He wanted to hold the rifle. I thought maybe he was going to go out hunting and get another rabbit or a squirrel or something. He was always so excitable. Up one minute, down the next. You never really knew where his feelings were going to veer off to next."

Joseph stood up and walked to the altar rail, where he stood listening to the sides of the church creak in response to the storm's throbbing pressure. When he finally turned to face his friends, tears flowed down his face.

"I'll never forget the sound of that rifle click echoing across the still river. Brett pointed it at me first. I thought he was joshing, then I realized he wanted to kill me. I guess I never knew until then how sick he was. How sad he was."

Peggy came up to him, taking his hands in hers. "What happened, Joseph?"

He took another deep breath. "He sat there like that for a minute. Then we argued about the girl some more. He accused me of encouraging her when I hadn't done any such thing." He laughed ruefully. "He said, 'You're what she wants—Mr. Perfect.' Like I was ever perfect at anything.

"He pulled up the rifle and turned it around, and I could see him working his thumb in around the trigger."

"Joseph, no. . . ." Otha Lee had moved to the front pew.

"I was sweating something awful, trying to edge up to him and not startle him. I begged him not to do it. He rubbed the tip of the barrel against his lips and said, 'Tell Ma and Pa I'm sorry.'" Joseph sat down heavily on the floor and looked up at Peggy. "I tried to stop him. I grabbed the rifle, but it went off and . . ." He buried his face in his hands, hiding his eyes as if he could hide the image of his brother's face disappearing, vanishing in an instant, along with twenty years of his own life. Vanished into tiny ripples in a torpid river on a sunny day in March.

"Then how come you to be put in prison, Joseph?" Otha Lee rubbed Joseph's shoulder.

"I don't understand that, either," Peggy said, drying her eyes. The storm's intensity had grown; the wind whistled solidly through the shutters.

Joseph sighed, pulling out a handkerchief and wiping his face. "Mama. I tried to explain what happened, but she wouldn't believe me. My own mama set the sheriff on me." He shrugged. "I think some folks believed me. I think maybe Papa did. But once Mama gets her mind set on something, ain't no setting it straight. I reckon it all makes some kind of strange sense now."

"Because she's not really your mother after all." Peggy moved closer and took his hand in hers.

Joseph looked at Peggy, then Otha Lee. "I can't believe y'all are taking this so calm. I figured once I told you, you'd run screaming."

"You've been a godsend—to me and Otha Lee," said Peggy. The old man nodded. "You've never given us any reason to believe you aren't the good and honorable man you've turned out to be."

"I knew something was chewing at you, son, but it wasn't up to me to pry it out of you." Otha Lee rubbed his chin and cocked his ear toward the rain pelting on the roof. "The truth's got a way of coming out in its own way, in its own time." He chuckled. "Seems like today was everybody's day of truth." He stood up and walked to another pew, where he knelt and prayed, his lips moving in silent supplication. Peggy and Joseph went to the back of the candlelit church and spoke quietly in the shadows.

"I'm sorry I didn't tell you sooner, Peggy. I thought about it a lot, but the time was never right."

"You needn't apologize. I did my own share of holding things back." She and Joseph stood close together. "Is that why you went to see your mother? Hoping to make things right again?"

"Yeah, but sometimes we can't ever make some things right again." He gently stroked her hair. "But that don't mean you can't make your troubles right. I hope you'll let me be there to help you."

Peggy looked up. "I'm going to get her back."

"I know you will. Can I ask you something?" Peggy nodded. "Do you know how I feel about you?"

She shook her head. "I don't know what you mean."

"I've been falling in love with you from the time you jumped ten feet in the air that day we met in the cemetery."

Peggy laughed. "Funny you should mention it. I don't think I started falling there. I think I just simply fell."

Joseph placed his hands on her shoulders. "I was thinking that if Gail gets her real mama back, you reckon she'd object to a new daddy?"

Peggy felt her eyes fill, and her voice collapsed to a whisper. "I never thought anyone would love me again."

"I always have, Peggy, and I always will. That's if you want me to."

Peggy nodded. "Yes, Joseph. I've always wanted you to."

The cemetery, nearly cleaned out the day before, now lay under a thick layer of tree limbs, leaves, branches, and a huge oak that split neatly through the middle, one half rolling to the west, covering the road, the other half falling to the east, felling all the gravestones in its path. Fortunately the church was untouched; only the roof was covered with debris but none that caused any damage.

"At least we're all in one piece," Joseph said, throwing limbs to one side, starting a new pile.

"I just wish I knew what happened to Otis," Otha Lee said wearily. None of them had slept for the howling winds and torrential rain.

Peggy ran to the house and returned with her car, maneuvering carefully around the fallen tree. "Joseph, take Otha Lee home and see if Otis might have gone back there."

Otha Lee was already easing into the passenger seat.

"You going to be okay here by yourself, Peggy?" Joseph put his arms around her.

"I'm better than I've been in years." She smiled as Joseph leaned down and kissed her gently on the lips.

Joseph and Otha Lee studied the nearly collapsed house for several minutes before noticing the pickup truck in the ditch across the road. Joseph ran over but found it empty.

"He must be around here somewhere," Joseph told Otha Lee, who had begun picking his way through the littered yard.

"Otis?" he shouted as he carefully climbed the steps. Joseph moved a piece of fallen porch roof so they could open the door. Inside, blue sky was visible through a gaping hole, and the living room was newly decorated with a combination of greenery and autumn leaves. "Otis," he shouted again.

A soft moan emanated from the corner of the room. Joseph and Otha Lee pulled away branches and found Otis laying partly concealed by an overturned chair.

"Son, are you all right?" Joseph and Otha Lee felt his body carefully; nothing appeared broken. Otis opened his eyes.

"Pops? Where've you been? I went looking all over for you." He sat up slowly and rubbed his forehead, which bore a large welt. "Pops, I wrecked the truck."

"Son, I don't care about any old truck. I have walked many a mile in my sorry life, and I 'spect I'll walk many more." He and Joseph helped Otis to his feet and took him into the kitchen, where at least the chairs were dry.

"We stayed in the church last night," Joseph said. "We wondered what became of you."

"I went to town to call my wife, but I got caught out in the storm. It was raining and blowing so hard when I came back, the truck slid off the road before I could do anything about it."

"Your wife?" Joseph said.

"More of that truth in its own time we were talking about last night," said Otha Lee, winking and rubbing Otis's shoulder.

Joseph nodded. "Looks like we're gonna have to rebuild your house again, Otha Lee."

He shook his head. "You done enough for me, and Miss Peggy, too. I got to find my own way this time." He came around the table and shook Joseph's hand. "You go on back to Miss Peggy. Me and Otis'll be just fine. Won't be the first time I slept under the stars. It might even turn out to be inspirational."

"If you say so. Take it easy, Otis."

"Yeah. Joseph?"

Joseph turned.

"Thanks for taking care of Pops." Otis glanced up at Otha Lee. "He's the only old man I got."

"You got him for good whether you want him or not," said Otha Lee, who was already clearing away the fallen leaves, as the sun shot a beam of light into the middle of his collapsed, but no longer broken, home.

Peggy walked up the aisle of the church. She was tired after the sleepless night but ready to get on with life. In the great scheme of things, Hurricane Hazel was a minor bump.

The church was unscathed. The candles had burned down to nubs; the sanctuary was still, quiet. Peggy knelt in front of the communion table.

"Dear Lord," she prayed. "Thank you for keeping us safe and for letting me find out what happened to my daughter. Please help me to tell her the truth so this legacy of lies can stop."

She lifted her eyes. "Thank you for Otha Lee, for his wisdom, courage, and friendship. Please look after him as he takes over the church. And thank you for Joseph. Thank you for letting me know again what it is to be loved and for giving me this wonderful person I can share my life with. Most of all, thank you for showing me the way back to faith. In Jesus' name . . ."

"Amen," came a voice from the rear of the church. Joseph.

Peggy jumped to her feet and laughed nervously. "I didn't know you were listening."

Joseph grinned. "Otha Lee better watch out or you'll be taking his job away."

"I doubt that," Peggy said, walking toward him.

Joseph looked around at the chapel's dim interior. "You know what we need?"

Peggy shook her head.

"A little light on the subject. Don't move." He ran outside.

So Peggy waited in the center aisle as he opened the shutters, one by one, and the sun gleamed through the stained-glass windows, bathing her in bands of rainbow light, until all the shutters had been opened, and the secrets were revealed, and Peggy knew, with certainty, that she and Joseph and Gail, and Otha Lee and maybe even Otis, would dwell in the house of the Lord. Forever and ever.

twenty-one

Otha Lee adjusted his bow tie in front of the bathroom mirror, joyfully whistling the tune to "We Gather Together." A cool breeze blew through the open window, heralding an Indian summer day, this Sunday before Thanksgiving. A splendid day for praise and worship. "God's timing is perfect," he declared, his voice echoing through the empty house. He thought back over the last few months, and marveled at how the summer had ended, how today was a new beginning for him and his congregation—perhaps for a few citizens of Bonham itself.

Otha Lee and Otis had spent nearly a week trying to put his house back together and had done a presentable job. Although the roof now sagged slightly, it did keep out the rain, and Otha Lee decided he could live without the porch, at least for the time being. He had spent far too much time sitting around fanning away gnats and mosquitoes instead of visiting his congregants and witnessing to the unconverted. Although he had spent the summer working on the Lord's house, he feared he had forgotten to attend to the Lord's work.

A man Otis had hired from the Bonham Garage had hauled the truck from the ditch. The damage turned out to be minimal, scratches and dings, at least leaving the truck in fair driving condition. Otha Lee and Otis had just gotten it back into the yard and were about to use a chain attached to the bumper to right the chicken coop—it had also blown over in the storm—when they heard a horn beeping down at the turnoff.

"Who can that be?" Otha Lee went to look down the road, Otis trailing behind. "Ain't seen nobody go by here since the storm."

He was startled to see Wycliffe, along with four other elders, pull up and spill out of his car, their expressions meek, yet somehow hopeful.

Wycliffe walked up to Otha Lee, extending his hand. "Brother Sturgis," he said, shaking the preacher's arthritic hand so firmly that Otha Lee thought he was going to have to holler "Uncle."

"Praise Jesus!" he cried, ignoring the pain and shaking each man's hand in turn. "I see the good Lord has spared us all."

"Indeed he has," said Wycliffe, placing a hand on Otha Lee's shoulder. "Indeed. His mercies are new every day."

Otis stood back, watching the exchange.

"What brings y'all by?" Otha Lee asked. "I just now got my truck out of the ditch over yonder, or I'd've been by to check on you, 'stead of the other way around."

"Penitence, Brother Sturgis," said Wycliffe, his eyes resting on Otha Lee's before glancing back at the waiting men. "There's something about a brush with nature's wrath that makes one look at one's actions. Sometimes it can even bring about a meeting of minds."

"Brother Wycliffe, I believe I'm going to put you up on the pulpit when next we meet again." Otha Lee laughed.

Wycliffe shook his head. "Our opposition to the new church building was wrongheaded, Otha Lee, just plain, out-and-out wrongheaded. Letting you and that hired man do all that work when we all had able bodies that could have moved the rebuilding along? When we could have saved Miss Peggy the trouble of clearing out that cemetery herself?"

"All things happen for a purpose, my friend," Otha Lee replied. "There were reasons each of us had the job we had to do. I believe we accomplished those jobs. And they were done in God's time. Y'all working with us wasn't part of the plan. Otherwise, me and Peggy and Joseph wouldn't have gone through what we needed to so we could get on with what else we've got to do in our lives."

"That may be true," Wycliffe said. "But the truth is, the hurricane has undone some of your work. The cemetery's a mess again, and the church hasn't even been painted. There's still a ways to go." He motioned the elders forward. "We've come to help you finish the job."

One by one, each man broke into a grin. Otha Lee glanced at Otis, who also smiled, tinkering beneath the truck's dented hood. "Are you all sure?" he said, silently giving a prayer of thanks.

"We come to get you," one man said.

"That's right," added Wycliffe. "If we want to be in that church come Thanksgiving, we better hustle! And besides," he chuckled, "the brush arbor's blowed to bits!"

"Go on, Pops," Otis said, wiping grease from his hands. "I'll have the coop standing again by the time you get back."

"Don't you want to come help us?" Otha Lee said, facing his son.

"I can't." He took a deep breath and ran his hand down his face. "I need to pack."

"You're going home?" He brightened at this last, although the fear crossed his mind that he might not see his son again.

"For a while."

"For a while? You mean you're coming back?"

"I was thinking about it, Pops. If I can put my marriage back together, I think it might be best if we all came back down here to live."

"What about the baby?" Otha Lee asked. "You know you got to take care of that new child you helped make."

Otis nodded. "I know. I plan to help raise him. Or her. It's not going to be easy, particularly if I come back here. I haven't quite got it all figured out yet. A lot's going to depend on my wife—whether she'll forgive me."

"There ain't any colleges around here nowhere. What'll you do to make a living?"

"I can still teach. Maybe at the colored high school."

"What about your book?"

Otis sighed and shook his head. "Writing about something and doing something are two different things. It's time I gave something back other than words." He laughed. "I guess some of your sermons are finally sinking in."

"Well, it's about time, son." He clapped his son on the shoulder. "It's about time."

At the church, the men threw themselves wholeheartedly and enthusiastically into the remaining work. Otha Lee could see the relief in Peggy's and Joseph's faces when they had driven up and assigned themselves to the remaining tasks. Two of the men worked on painting the church's interior, while two more cleared debris from the cemetery, and Wycliffe helped Joseph refinish the remaining pews. They had been working for a couple of hours when another car full of men arrived. Peggy was walking through the cemetery balancing a tray filled with tall glasses of lemonade when she saw it stop. Her heart skipped a beat, and she called out to Joseph, who ran from the church, while Otha Lee froze, recognizing the man behind the wheel, recalling the night long before that had changed his life forever.

Mr. Grosvenor got out, along with three other men that Peggy recognized from her father's business dealings and his position as deacon at the First Baptist Church.

The hardware dealer took off his hat and gestured toward the church. "Y'all doing a fine job on this old building," he said, walking around and admiring the paint job in progress. Otha Lee held his breath, waiting for another car to arrive—there was always more than one carful, that he knew—but none came. Mr. Grosvenor walked over to Otha Lee and Peggy, who had managed to place the tray on the steps, worried it might fall from her shaking hands.

He cleared his throat. "Miss Peggy, I knew your daddy from way back. I guess you know that."

Peggy nodded, folding her arms.

"We grew up in a different time and place. We didn't truck with associating with coloreds." He fiddled with his hat before looking at Otha Lee. "At least I didn't, anyhow. When I heard about you giving Otha Lee here this church, it didn't set right somehow. It kinda went in the face of everything I grew up believing and feeling. White churches belong to whites and colored belong to coloreds."

"Is this going somewhere?" Peggy rolled their telephone conversation over in her mind and tried to remember anything her father ever said about Mr. Grosvenor, then realized she had never heard him mention his name. Otha Lee, on the other hand, remembered his deed but said nothing, not wanting Peggy to know what her father had done. She already knew quite enough.

Mr. Grosvenor stepped toward Otha Lee, who met him step-for-step.

"Have you got something to say to me?" He looked Mr. Grosvenor square in the eye, something he had never done before. He decided now was a good time to start.

"We've come to help you. Finish the church, I mean." He met Otha Lee's stare. "I'm thinking maybe I was wrong about a few things. Maybe more than a few things. It's long overdue that I gave something back, instead of taking away."

"Yes, it is," said Otha Lee, nodding in agreement, the image of a man in a white hood giving way to the reality of the contrite soul standing before him. "Wycliffe, would you show these men what needs doing?"

"Brother Sturgis?" Wycliffe looked at the men with trepidation. The other elders held back, eyeing the men suspiciously.

Otha Lee held out his hand to Mr. Grosvenor, who shook it gently and cast his eyes to the ground. "It's all right. This man knows what he's doing."

The men hesitated, then followed Wycliffe inside the building. Peggy came over to Otha Lee. "What was that all about? You know he wouldn't let us have credit to buy the supplies."

"I know, Miss Peggy. But holding grudges don't hurt anybody 'cept the one holding it." He laughed. "Besides, we need the help." He kept on laughing, much to Peggy's confusion.

"Otha Lee, what's come over you?"

"Oh, I was just thinking. I'm thinking maybe we need to have a hurricane blow through here more often."

"Oh," Peggy said, looking around at the accumulated debris. "Why is that?"

"Seems to go a lot further toward changing souls than any sermon I could ever preach."

Otha Lee stood in the central hall of the manse. The manse where he would live out his remaining days. The manse that once belonged to Peggy was now the property of the Mount Gilead Missionary Baptist Church, along with the cemetery and church building itself.

The morning before, Peggy and Joseph had come by his house, along with the men—colored and white—who had completed their assigned jobs. Peggy had handed him two documents bound in blue paper. "I believe these are yours," she said, backing away. He opened the one on top, the deed to the church, before opening the second.

He read the document, bewildered at the words that swirled across the crisp paper. "Miss Peggy!" He refolded the deed and pushed it toward her with a trembling hand. "You can't give me your house."

"Yes, I can, and I *am* giving it to you. The church minister can't be living half a county away from his church." She smiled and slid her fingers across Joseph's calloused palm. "We moved my things yesterday. I've rented a house in town until we are married and can build our own. We're here to help you move."

Otha Lee felt faint, so he sat on the porch. Even the cool November air didn't seem to help. He put his head in his hands to hide the tears that welled in his eyes. Joseph came and placed his hand gently on the old preacher's back.

"She means it, Otha Lee," he whispered, "and you know how she is when she means something."

Otha Lee recovered himself and smiled at Peggy, who had come to stand beside her husband-to-be. "The church was more than I ever hoped for, but the house, too. Miss Peggy, I just don't know what to say."

"You don't have to say anything." She took Otha Lee's hand. "Just promise me you'll enjoy it for the rest of your life."

"That, I can say, Miss Peggy. I promise. And we'll take good care of it all, won't we, brothers?"

"Yes, indeed," said Wycliffe, bringing a chair from the parlor and placing it carefully in the back of Otha Lee's truck.

"But I think we're going to need a bigger truck," said Joseph. Otha Lee looked around at his meager assortment of possessions. "Why do you say that?"

"Because we ain't got nearly enough room for all them pigs."

"I can't believe my daughter is coming home this weekend," Peggy exclaimed, letting Joseph spin her among the unpacked moving boxes in the living room. Laughing like kids, they collapsed on the sofa.

"It's good to see you so happy, Peggy," Joseph said, pulling her into his arms. It was nearly time to head out to church, but he and Peggy had been so caught up in getting her moved into the rented house that they hadn't had time to relax. "I never thought I'd love anyone as much as I love you. And after we get married, I'm gonna be the best daddy in the world."

"Does that come with a guarantee?" Peggy smiled and snuggled against him, heedless of getting her Sunday dress wrinkled.

"Bona fide for my future bride."

Peggy couldn't remember ever feeling so jubilant. Gail would be coming home, and not to Eva. To her. Amid all the legal wrangling, Peggy had agreed to let Gail remain at boarding school until Thanksgiving. Her daughter would be allowed one last day with Eva, then she would be told the truth. Peggy knew it wouldn't be an easy thing for Gail to learn. She was well aware of what it was like to be lied to by so many people, and for so long; she and Gail had a strong bond, however, one not only of blood but of love and faith. And the bond extended to Joseph as well, whom she trusted to help her give her daughter—and the children they planned to have together—a good home where love was not a matter of feeling but of expression and joy.

Suddenly Joseph jumped up. "Peggy, we're gonna be late for Otha Lee's sermon!"

She glanced at the clock. "Oh, my goodness. Where's my hat?" She grabbed it from the hall table, giving the pot of yellow chrysanthemums a quick adjustment while Joseph opened the door, only to find Beatrice and Belva standing on the other side, dressed in bright orange silk shantung dresses, looking for all the world like two svelte pumpkins.

"I'm so glad we caught you . . . ," said Belva.

"Before you left for church," said Beatrice.

"We're running late, ladies," Joseph chimed in, closing the door behind Peggy.

"I didn't expect to see you," Peggy said. It had been a while since she had seen any of her sisters outside of a lawyer's office. She hated that it had come to that.

"We came to apologize," Belva said, pulling at her purse handle. "We knew the truth for so long, and we kept it from you, and it's just unforgivable. We know better, and we let Eva run all over us and, and, I don't know what to say, Peggy, I just don't know."

"We want to say that we hope you can find it in your heart to forgive us." Beatrice took Peggy's hand. "We know Eva betrayed you terribly. Having lost children of our own, we should have known better than to go along with such a scheme. But the past is gone. There's nothing we can change about that."

"We were just hoping maybe we could change the future," Belva added, taking Peggy's other hand.

Peggy searched her sisters' faces, seeing their contrition, and realized that she no longer felt any anger toward them. "I do forgive you. I've been so caught up in just trying to get Gail back here with me that I'm afraid I didn't stop to think about what this had done to us."

Beatrice dabbed at her eyes with a lace handkerchief. "I know it's not enough, but maybe it will be a start. Will you please come have Thanksgiving dinner with us? And you, too, Joseph, of course."

Peggy considered for a few seconds. "Will Eva be there?" Her voice was quiet but firm.

Belva shook her head. "No." The twins exchanged glances. "No Thanksgiving dinner. No brunches. I suppose it's going to take us all a long time to forgive Eva."

Peggy knew Belva was right. She wondered if she would ever be able to put the betrayal behind her. She knew she had to in order to heal, but sometimes forgiveness doesn't come easily, especially when the hurt is so deep, so personal. And when the time came, Peggy knew she would probably have to be the one to take the first step. Perhaps time would change Eva's heart, and she would see the damage she had done. Peggy wondered if that could ever happen. Maybe then reconciling would be easier, and the sisters would be a true family, not just people who happen to be related by blood.

"The important thing is that Gail is coming home—home to you where she belongs," Beatrice said, looping her arm through Belva's. "So will you come for Thanksgiving dinner?"

"I'd love to," Peggy said, hugging the twins, one in each arm, knowing that although one relationship had been severed, others would grow stronger and deeper, secure now, in a haven of unquestionable truth.

The golden morning light cast a glow across the stately monuments commemorating the history of the church. As he strode through the cemetery, Otha Lee paused and reflected on the names, remembering the faces and voices, grateful that their legacy of belief and faith would now become that of his own congregation. The old slave section, a quiet plain of unmarked graves, bore testament to another legacy, one he acknowledged as he knelt and prayed for God's guidance toward a way of peace and understanding, for himself and those now living.

He entered the church and beheld the polished mahogany pulpit, the carving of Moses and the Israelites, and the windows, shimmering and iridescent, telling the great Bible stories wordlessly, resplendently.

His congregation arrived, and he stood at the door, welcoming them into their new church home. They exclaimed over the spacious sanctuary, redolent with new paint and varnish, adorned with the windows borne of a pure and loving heart, proclaiming the miracles of a greater glory.

Miss Douglas walked through the back door and threw her hands into the air. "Praise God in all his glory!" she cried, grabbing people at random and giving them bear hugs. "I ain't never seen such a beautiful church in all my natural born life."

Otha Lee smiled and suppressed an urge to run around hugging people himself. He turned to see Roy arrive, his expression dubious, but fading to awe as he joined the rest of the congregation in their unabashed gazes of admiration.

Returning to the altar, he saw Peggy and Joseph enter and seat themselves on the back row. Otha Lee grasped the sides of the pulpit and welcomed the gathered faithful.

"Thursday may be Thanksgiving, my friends," he began, opening his Bible. "But if y'all don't mind, I think we'll start the celebration a few days early."